ACE
POST MORTEM
TWIST

WYLD ENCHANTMENT WOODS
COZY MYSTERY

Kura Jane Carpenter

WUP

Wicked Unicorn Press

Dedication:

To **Kay Mercer,
Angela Oliver,**
and **Alice Carpenter**

~ My Fantastic
Beta Readers!

Published by **Wicked Unicorn Press**

National Library of New Zealand Cataloguing-in-Publication Data
Ace Post Mortem Twist / Kura Jane Carpenter
ebook ISBN   978-1-99-117728-5
softcover ISBN   978-1-99-117729-2

MAP OF ELLA'S HOME

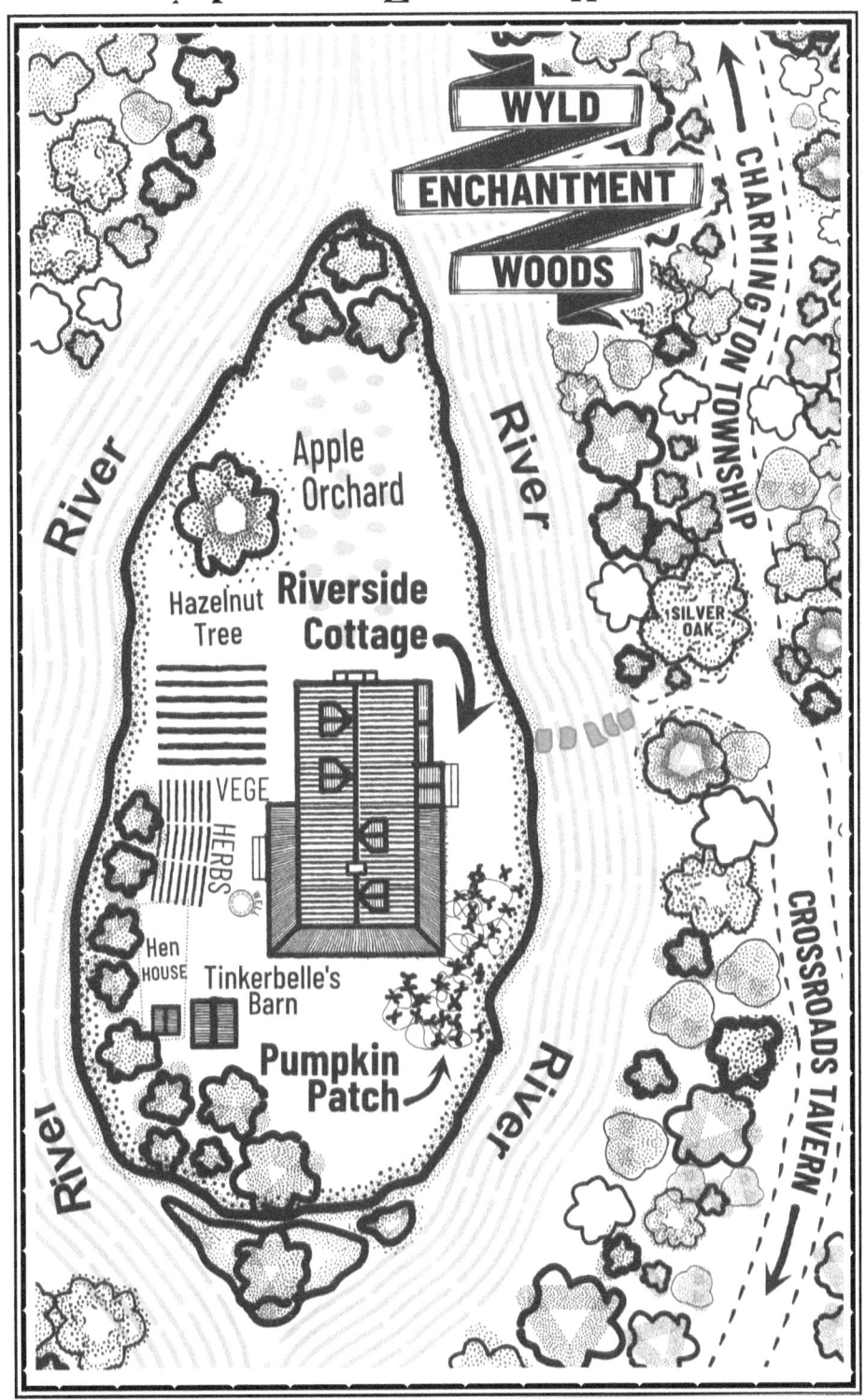

CHARMINGTON TO NOTTINGHAM

CONTENTS

Cast of Characters

- **Ella Charming** – Former Fairy Godmother – Sister of the Queen.
- **Tom April** – Rookie Castle Guardsman - Accidentally swapped bodies with Ella's cat.
- Ace – Engineer on the night watch.
- Axel Luther – Sheriff of Charmington township.
- Baker Street Boys: Olly, Sam, Sandy – Orphan children.
- Bron the Baker – Proprietor of Southgate Bakery.
- Cassidy Turpin – head of the night watch – Niece of Dirk.
- Cheapcuts / Chelton Junior – Son of Martha and Chelton.
- Chelton – Butcher – Husband of Martha.
- Cinderella (deceased) – Princess – Sister of Ella and Sibylla.
- Dirk Turpin – Royal coachman – Uncle of Cassidy Turpin.
- Doctor Edison Hyde – Doctor at the Hot Cockle Land Hospital .
- Goldilocks – Royal hairdresser.
- Gretel – Millennial – Sister of Hansel.
- Hansel – Millennial – Brother of Gretel.
- Harold Harper – Postmaster – Father of Hillary.
- Hillary Harper – Post office clerk – Daughter of Harold.
- Katie – Former Barmaid at the Gatehouse Inn.
- Marge – Midwife – A notorious gossip.
- Martha Chelton – Wife of Chelton the butcher.
- Master Spicer – Cook at the Nottingham Home for Unwanted Boys.
- Merlin – Famous Magician – Brother to Ella & Sibylla, lives in Avalon.
- Millie – Haberdashery owner – Twin sister of Sally.
- Mistress Fairweather – Matron of the Baker Street orphanage.
- Mr Beau – Shoeshine man, also maintains the streetlamps.
- Mr Puddles – Willow's pet poodle.
- Mrs Haversham – Former headmistress of the Haversham Academy.
- Nigella Pickford – Actress.
- Prince John – Regent of Sherwood.
- Richard – Woodcutter – Husband of Cinderella.
- Robinne Scarlett – Brewer at the Crossroads Tavern.
- Rooster – A Nottingham criminal.
- Red Unicorn – A Charmington Folkhero and Outlaw.
- Rum (deceased) – Former proprietor of the Crossroads Tavern.
- Sally – Haberdashery owner – Twin sister of Millie.
- Sebastian – Charmington's Mayor.
- Sibylla – Queen of Wyld Kingdom – Twin sister of Ella.
- Sisters Grimm – Authors of the popular novel *Cinderella*.
- Tilly – Ella's cat.
- Tobias – School Master – Aspiring romance novelist.
- Willow – Baker and witch.
- Wulf – Bodyguard to Prince John.

CHAPTER 1

ELLA IS SET UP

"Tax collector?" Ella blinked at the Charmington council members gathered for their early morning meeting. "You want me to be the town's tax collector?" Surely, they were joking.

"On the contrary. *I* do not want *you* to be the tax collector," began Harold Harper, the postmaster, while from somewhere in the ceiling above in the town hall clock, the mechanical roosters crowed seven, "however, Queen Sibylla has impressed upon us *someone* must collect rents and taxes."

Never in all her days did Ella expect to find herself agreeing with Harold. Ever since he had falsely assumed that he was something of a catch and she should be grateful for his attention, they had not seen eye-to-eye. But on this madness, they could agree.

Someone had to collect taxes.

How many of the six other people gathered here knew the true financial crisis their small woodland kingdom was facing due to the ban of magic in a town that had built its economy on magic?

"But Sibylla didn't say anything about collecting taxes...." *But everyone will hate me more than they already do!* was what Ella really wanted to say, but instead she added a rather deflated, "Sibylla asked me to help oversee the rental increases."

"It's the same job. The rents *are* our main form of tax collection. Really, have you always been this dim?" Harold threw his hands up. "Shall I beg the queen for a new candidate?"

"Ignore Harold, we all agree you're perfect for the job," said Sally, the local haberdashery owner. She and her twin sister Millie were the town council's duly elected business representatives. Sally patted Ella's hand, and raised her chin to address Goldilocks, who was perched at the head of the table in a custom highchair that accommodated her small size. "Don't we, Goldilocks? Everyone knows Lady Ella is kind. She would never lock someone out of their home and leave them in the cold, unlike others I could name."

To Ella's left, Millie, Sally's twin, stiffened. Her elderly wrinkled hand clenched into a fist around a lavender-scented lace handkerchief.

Tucking a strand of her expertly styled bouffant hairdo behind an ear, Goldilocks, who was minuting the meeting with a bright-pink ostrich feather quill, looked up from her page of notes and nodded brightly. "Absolutely. We all want you on board. Isn't that right, Mr. Mayor?"

There was no reply from the mayor, which was unsurprising because he was asleep.

Goldilocks discreetly nudged the sleeping mayor beside her with her patent leather pumps. The elderly man didn't respond. His chin had sunken onto his chest. Thin strands of white hair had flopped unkempt over his face, abandoning their assigned duty to hide his baldness.

Across the table, sitting closest to the large window overlooking the picturesque Northgate Square buildings dusted with a coating of snow, the newly appointed town sheriff, Axel Luther, yawned and rocked back on his chair. A sly grin spread across his angular features. "I guess the votes will determine the outcome."

"Votes?" Ella found herself saying, not out of concern, but surprise.

"Aww, didn't you know there's still a vote?" Axel intoned mockingly. He thumped the heels of his boots upon the tabletop and crossed his arms across his broad chest, yawning again. "I wonder how I shall vote? Hmm?"

Ella thinned her lips. "Keep your vote. I would much rather not have the backing of a murderer, thank you very much."

"Alleged murderer," Axel growled. But then winked. "No one *saw* me do it."

He might be less smug if he had any idea his new and expensive-looking boots had a large green stain across the soles. No doubt a paint spill from the renovations he had undertaken in the last week making over the former Gatehouse Inn into his new headquarters. Now there was a crime! Turning Arthur's beloved café business into a police station.

Millie, who had been squishing her handkerchief into an ever-increasingly smaller ball, snapped, "If you must be up all night *yee-hawing* over your promotion, that's your business, but show some respect! Take your filthy feet off the table!"

Ella sat back, startled by Millie's outburst. She had seldom heard the shopkeeper raise her voice.

With the grudging exaggeration a teenager might display rather than a man in his mid-thirties, Axel thumped his booted feet onto the council chamber floor.

Harold Harper coughed and smoothed his silk cravat and matching bland grey vest. "Shall we cast the votes, then? All in favour of Ella Charming being appointed onto the council in the official role of—"

"Wait!" Goldilocks cried. Dropping her pink ostrich feather quill and scooting off her highchair, she leapt down from the tall table. "Sorry, everyone," the minuscule woman said, "I have to nip to the bathroom! Back in a tick."

Harold and Axel rolled their eyes, and Ella took a breath. It certainly wasn't as if she *wanted* to be the tax collector.

After all, the position would be a huge drain on her time. Time she could be devoting to helping her lodger, young Tom April, focus on the task of turning back into a human after an unfortunate magical accident in which he had swapped bodies with Ella's cat. Certainly, Ella would like her cat back just as much as young Tom would like his life back.

"Allow me to refresh your teacup, your ladyship," Sally said at Ella's side.

At the same moment, Millie pushed back her chair and raced to claim the tea urn on the sideboard. "No, allow me. I know exactly how you like it with just a drop of honey. Sally is too heavy-handed!"

What was up with the two sisters? Usually, they were like two sides of the same coin. And in the decades Ella had known the haberdashery twins, this was the first time she had ever seen them wearing outfits that did *not* match. Even their accessories hanging on the coat rack near the door seemed purposefully chosen to clash. Never had there been a more passive-aggressive display from a coat rack than Sally's butterscotch-yellow clutch purse and Millie's lime-green parasol.

Ella cast her mind back, trying to recall the last time she'd seen them together. Was it when rumours of a werewolf infection had induced panic among the citizens? Yes...and Millie had accused Sally of being infected.

"Do you mind checking on Sebastian?" Harold said to Axel, who was sitting closest to the mayor at the head of the grand old oak table. "He's not dead, is he?"

Axel reached across the table and grabbed Goldilocks' ostrich feather, then proceeded to poke Sebastian's beakish nose. "Dead drunk...sleeping off last night. Speaking of... Where were you last night, Harold? You missed out on a good time."

"I don't drink," Harold muttered haughtily. "Besides, I hardly think it would be fitting for a man of my station to attend such a raucous event. There are bottles on the town hall steps!"

A light tap on the door was followed by a young woman with a brunette pixie haircut tentatively peeking around the chamber door. Hillary Harper, Harold's daughter. Seeing the council members were taking a break, she entered the room and gently closed the door. "Ahh, Dad, can I borrow your key? I can't open the post office, and people are waiting outside."

"Postmaster, when we're at work, refer to me as *Postmaster*," he corrected peevishly, reaching into his pocket and drawing out a thin brass key on a shiny length of chain. "This is very inconvenient. Mine is attached to my waistcoat! Did you forget yours?"

Hillary wrung her hands and didn't meet anyone's eye. "I lost it."

"What? Again? That's the second key this month!" bellowed Harold, his pasty complexion developing two red spots on his cheeks that clashed horribly with the unusual shade of brown he had dyed his hair.

Really, did he think he was fooling anyone with that dye job? It looked as solid and unnatural as a helmet. Maybe it was a wig? Ella found herself thinking as Harold stood up and struggled to undo his vest's shiny brass buttons. The fitted garment was much tighter than it looked.

"I fell asleep at my desk last night," Hillary explained, rubbing her face, "and when I went outside, the streetlamps weren't working."

Ella felt a twinge of sympathy. The poor girl had bags under her eyes. Clearly, Harold worked her too hard. Odious man.

"It was very dark," Hillary continued. "I must have dropped the key somewhere between the back door of the post office and my lodgings. I tripped over a couple of times..."

From over at the sideboard where she was prepping the tea, Millie piped up, "Indeed, it *was* very dark—young Hillary and Axel's blundering around in the alley outside my window woke me up. I loaned them a lantern and instructed Axel to walk her home." She crossed her arms tightly and scowled at Axel as if to say she would not forget the loan. "I shall have a very strong word with Mr. Beau when next I see him—he's responsible for maintaining the streetlamps. They were lit when I went to bed! Imagine if they'd gone out when that werewolf was loose last month?" She turned as if to seek backup from her sister, momentarily forgetting they were arguing.

"Well, sir, you have my thanks for seeing my daughter home safely," Harold said grudgingly to Axel, and he held out the waistcoat with its attached post office key for Hillary.

My goodness, Ella thought, eyeing the faint outline under Harold's white shirt. Was he wearing a *corset* under his clothes? How very vain.

Axel yawned and mumbled something about just doing his civic duty when Hillary, from under her fringe, shared a secret smile with him. Hillary grabbed the offered key and waistcoat and scuttled out of the chambers.

Magic preserve! Ella was stunned. That smile! Whatever did it mean? Were the pair in a relationship? Axel was a bit of a rogue, but *surely*, he wouldn't chase a girl barely out of her teens. Would he? Then again, he had been having an affair with the baker's young wife, so lacking morals was part of his *modus operandi*. Although Ginny at least had been closer to his own age...

Ella's musings were interrupted as the door opened again, and who should it be, not Goldilocks returning, but Ella's sister, Queen Sibylla, dressed to kill, as she always was.

With a swift intake of breath, Harold was on his feet again in a trice, his blushing as furious as his profusion of greeting. "Marm! What an honour. We were about to vote." He cast an angry glance at the door. "If that wretched craftswoman would ever get back to her duty!" Turning away, he saw that the mayor wasn't on his feet and was now sagging over the table, his shiny balding head touching the tabletop. Harold stamped his foot. "Sebastian, wake up, man! Give the queen your chair!"

"Don't get up, don't get up," Sibylla trilled magnanimously and waved off the offer with an elegant flick of her blood-red painted fingernails. "Pretend I'm not here. I'll just take your seat, Harold," she said, gliding into the only vacant seat other than Goldilocks' little highchair. "I've just come to see *democracy* in action. Ladies, don't you look beautiful? And Axel, have I congratulated you on your promotion?" Her full lips parted in a toothy smile.

Ella pressed her own lips firmly together as the council members made small talk and once again extolled Axel's virtues and suitability in the new role as town sheriff. He had previously been the head of the castle guards—or head of the henchmen, as the majority of the townsfolk referred to him. "What can I say?" Axel answered with false modesty and an off-handed, one-shouldered shrug, as if he wasn't lapping up every ounce of praise. "Criminals are my forte."

"Takes one to know one," Ella whispered under her breath.

Sibylla arched an eyebrow at her sister and cast a stern look as if about to say something cutting, but Goldilocks reappeared. She bobbed a curtsey to Sibylla, and then climbed the steps to her seat and clasped her pink quill once more. "Sorry, everyone. Where were we?" She dipped her quill into the ink and looked expectantly at their faces.

"Oh, yes, well," blustered Harold, self-consciously running his hand over his exposed shirtfront. "Yes, ahem. All in favour of Ella Charming being appointed onto the council in the official role of tax collector? Raise your hand and say 'Aye.'"

Harold's hand was up before he had finished speaking, and Ella had to physically stop herself from groaning out loud at his toadying turnaround. He really was the worst.

"Aye!" cried Sally and Millie, their hands up so fast it could have been a competition.

Everyone looked expectantly at Axel, who pointedly adjusted his sleeve cuffs and then sat on his hands.

"Three against one, and one, er, abstained," Harold said with barely a pause to account for the sleeping mayor. "The ayes have it. Now if everyone can forgive me, I'll duck out early and assist Hillary." Clutching his stomach, he flourished a formal bow to the queen and exited the room.

What a toad, Ella thought, and then regarded her sister. If Sibylla had expected Axel to vote according to her wishes, she betrayed no trace of annoyance on her smooth and deceptively youthful features. Sibylla clapped her hands and turned to Ella, saying, "How delightful to see the Charmington council in action. Like an efficient machine, each member a valued cog."

Cogs, were they? Ella held back a retort. If they were a machine, it was Sibylla cranking the handle. Clearly, her presence had influenced Harold's vote.

"Tax collector?" Ella crossed her arms and glared at her sister. "You set me up."

CHAPTER 2

LAWBREAKER

"Nonsense, Sister dear. As to the title, fret not. On official documents, you will be referred to as the tax collector, but in day-to-day duties, we've found citizens are much more responsive if we describe the role as 'Administrative Director of Rent and Repairs.'" Sibylla grinned like a cat with a mouse.

"Repairs too? Hmm," Ella muttered. "Why stop there? Perhaps I can scrub doorsteps and feed pets."

The queen cocked her head. "You did say you would help. Do whatever it takes," Sibylla said, reminding Ella of her promise last month.

Ella couldn't argue there. She and Sibylla might not see eye-to-eye, but they could put their differences aside and work for the best outcome for their town. The brink of financial ruin! It didn't bear thinking about.

"You'll be perfect—you move with all *levels* of society."

Or in other words, levels which Sibylla felt were beneath her.

"We all agree Lady Ella is perfect for the job. I was just saying to Goldilocks earlier how Lady Ella is kind and fair, and most importantly *loyal*," Sally added with a sidelong glance at Millie.

"Indeed, hardworking too," Millie responded quickly and began clearing away the teacups. "Not the kind of person to take credit for another's work. Always does her fair share." She left Sally's cup on the table.

Sibylla was already standing up and not paying the haberdashery sisters' bickering any attention. "Goldilocks will show you to your office and fill you in on the role," she told Ella.

"Why bother staging a vote if you rig the outcome?" Ella asked as her sister was vacating the room in a swish of shimmering taffeta skirts with gold flecks on royal purple.

"Rigging the vote? How hurtful!" Sibylla threw a glance over her shoulder. Despite her comment, she was grinning ear-to-ear in much the same fashion she had when she watched Ella being stripped of her magical powers and having her wand snapped.

Clearly, her sister had some larger scheme afoot...

Ella got to her feet as Goldilocks shuffled her papers in order. Beside her, the mayor remained in his relaxed state of oblivion, only now, Axel had joined him. Quietly nodding off in the warm room—after a very late-night partying and who knows what else—while outside the window, snowflakes swirled about like confetti.

"Allow me to assist," Sally said, fetching Ella's black woollen cloak from the coat rack—while managing to knock Millie's lime-green parasol to the floorboards at the same time—then draping the cloak across Ella's shoulders.

"And your cane," Millie added, gathering up the walking stick propped by the door, and in a similar bout of clumsiness, somehow unhooking Sally's purse from the rack and standing on it as she passed the stick to Ella. "It's so elegant. Really sets off your whole outfit."

"Thank you, ladies," Ella replied, wondering if someone should wake the mayor.

As if reading her mind, Goldilocks hitched a thumb at the sleeping mayor and sheriff. "Last one out wakes the mayor. It's tradition."

Who am I to interfere with tradition? Ella thought, gesturing for the other ladies to exit the chambers before her.

Ella gripped her cane. It was well-known she was no great proponent of maintaining pointless protocol like who should leave first. But more than that, insisting the ladies leave first gave her knees a little more time to adjust to being upright and prepare for the walking ahead once more.

At least the town hall chambers and all the connecting corridors were pleasantly warm thanks to the innovative central heating system developed many decades ago by craftsmen in the employ of the crown. Indeed, those crafty individuals wouldn't have baulked at being in charge of 'and repairs.' That was exactly the kind of problem they had enjoyed solving.

Come to think of it, she had met a craftsman recently. Perhaps he might prove a useful addition to her tax team. What was his name?

He had repaired her walking stick—the light of which hadn't functioned in many years—and was now something she relied on with all the jaunts back and forth between the township and her own little cottage within the heart of Wyld Enchantment Woods.

Ace! That was his name. Ace and that clever guardswoman, Cassidy Turpin, the one Tom had a crush on, worked for the night watch. Perhaps the pair of them would like to join the tax collecting team? No, probably not...

"Don't be mad at Sibylla. I'm the one who suggested you for this role," Goldilocks said, beaming.

"What? You set me up? But why, Goldi?"

"Because you're kind and you care about the people! Now, stop looking for ulterior motives." Goldie handed over a golden length of chain with a wax seal shaped like a unicorn. "Your official insignia. Just pop it around your neck, that's right. Shall we go see your office first, or would you like the grand tour of the town hall?"

"Whichever route involves going up fewer stairs suits me best," Ella told the little craftswoman and lifted her walking stick to emphasise the point.

Goldilocks winced in sympathy. "Knees playing up?"

Ella nodded. "You, my dear, are one of the few privileged to know my—and my sister's—true age. Magic keeps Sibylla together, but with my powers stripped, I feel *every* century." Ella held up a hand before the other woman could respond. "Ignore my complaining. I'll survive. I was just thinking, Charmington has endured two decades of non-stop winter, and yet, the central heating system in the town hall holds together. I am sure I will too. Were your ancestors involved in the hall's construction? It really is a magnificent work of craftsmanship."

Goldilocks blushed and held her ostrich quill to her nose, as if to hide her smile. "You old flatterer, you!" She pointed with the bright pink feather to a large chandelier that overhung the staircase. "My great-great-uncle devised all the light fittings. If you squint, you can see they have the same unicorn motifs as your chain."

Ella found herself doing just that and peered up at the elaborate brass construction that beamed light into the spiralling steps below. Goldilocks sneezed and dropped her feather. Bending to reach it, she muttered, "One, two, three," and tapped Ella's boot toe.

A vibration zipped up through Ella's body, and the dull ache that constantly radiated from her knees vanished like a candle flame puffing out. "Goldi! You mustn't waste your magic on me."

The little woman tapped a finger to her lips. "Magic is banned, and I am positively hurt that you think I would break the law." But her smile said otherwise.

A male voice enquired from behind the pair, "Who's breaking the law?"

CHAPTER 3

HOW MANY DEAD BODIES?

TOWN HALL, CHARMINGTON.

"I believe you are," Ella said with a smile, turning towards the white fluffy cat slinking down the hall toward them. "Being a talking cat probably ranks highly in magical misdemeanours." She placed a hand on her hip. "Tom, didn't you promise that if I let you come with me into town today, you wouldn't utter a word?"

Tomcat sat and his tail flicked. "Er... It was a bet. Not a promise." He ducked his little cat head. Somehow, he looked remarkably sheepish for a feline.

Goldilocks, in the meantime, shut her mouth. It had hung open when she realised the cat was indeed talking to them. "Saints alive! How did you spell your cat to talk if you can't fix your own knees?"

"It's a long story," Ella began.

"I wished on a star!" said Tom, blinking emerald-green cat eyes.

"Maybe not so long," Ella muttered with a sigh. "Lead on, Goldilocks..." She tucked her cane under her arm, realising she didn't need the stick's support. "Magic preserve! Are we going up or down the stairs? All of a sudden, I'm looking forward to this!"

"Up. The tax office is in the town hall attic. And I'm afraid the pain-fade won't last. A week at the most, I'm sorry."

"Don't be sorry. You have given me a gift, and I shall enjoy every moment." Not waiting for the other two, she set off up the staircase.

IF ELLA HAD BEEN TOLD a week ago that the office for the role she'd unwittingly taken on was at the very top of the town hall, located in the sprawling attic offices, she probably would have refused the position. But this morning, thanks to Goldi's magical healing abilities, she practically raced up the stairs.

Flushed and more than a little out of breath, Ella arrived at her new office to find she wasn't the first to the door. Millie, one of the elderly haberdashery twins, still wringing her lace hanky and dressed in her passive-aggressive lime-green finery, stood up from the bench seat in the hall. She bobbed a curtsey and plastered a smile across her weathered features, but Ella had seen the look of perplexity creasing Millie's brow when she had raced up the last of the stairs.

"My first enquiry, I take it?" Ella said cheerfully, hoping to set the elderly lady at her ease. "What can I do for you, rental or repairs?"

"It's a matter of some delicacy..." Millie began as Goldilocks and Tomcat rushed up the stairs behind Ella.

"Discretion is my middle name, I assure you," Ella said, casting a warning glance at Tom that she hoped he would interpret as, *'Act like a cat! And not like a man trapped in a cat's body.'*

Thankfully, he leapt up onto the windowsill of the small round window at the top of the stairs to admire the view of the snow-draped town square far below.

"My middle name is Penelope," said Goldilocks, "But have no fear. I'm a strongbox of Sibylla's secrets, and I'm sure yours pale in comparison."

Millie continued to torture the lavender-scented lace handkerchief between her wrinkled hands. "It's just with the upcoming rental increases—which I have no objection to, of course. It's just, I got to thinking about the tenancy agreement that my sister and I signed. Well, it was so long ago, I can't remember. Did Sally actually sign it?" She turned away, and Goldi shared a sharp look with Ella.

Goodness! Could the haberdashery sisters' quarrel be that serious? Was Millie looking for a way to force Sally out of their business partnership?

"I completely understand," Ella replied, while not really understanding at all. But that was beside the point. She had told Sibylla she could handle this role, and that she would help in whatever way she could. Keeping the citizens of Charmington happy was her priority. That much she did understand. "Do you know where the original documents are kept?" She asked this last part to Goldilocks.

"All the really old records—I mean, the *important* tenancy agreements signed more than fifty years ago—are in basement storage," Goldilocks answered, and Millie sagged a little, as if realising her simple request might not be so simply resolved.

"Leave it with us," Ella said in a soothing tone. "I will look into it personally and aim to deliver the information you require by the end of the day. I'll come by the haberdashery. Don't fret, I will only speak directly to you on the matter."

Millie released her stranglehold on the hanky and folded the lace cloth away into a lime-green coat pocket as if a weight had been lifted from her mind. "Thank you, Lady Ella, that is most accommodating of you. I am grateful." Her worried expression dissipated, and she added as an afterthought, "Perhaps you both would care for some afternoon tea? And do bring your lovely cat. I have been meaning to make a new bow for him." She paused to give Tomcat a pat before proceeding back down the stairs, her demeanour much now like Ella's own after Goldi had removed her pain and she had been given a new lease on life.

Ella waited a few moments before sighing. "We're going to get dusty scrambling around in the basement hunting for those records, aren't we? Thank the stars you tweaked my knees. I already have a feeling this job will be the death of me."

"No hunting required," Goldi assured. "The trouble is we'll have to get permission, and the key, from one of the post office staff."

"Ugh. You mean on my first day I have to go begging for a favour from Harold? Worst luck."

"It's probably easier if I go do it," Goldi offered. "I know exactly where those old rental records are because I helped move them. There was a burst pipe last month, and all the records were put in temporary storage on the post office's side of the shared basement level."

Ella shook her head. "Very kind, but I'm going to have to get used to working with him." She turned to Tom, who was still peering out the window. "Are you coming?"

"I'll catch up. Did you know you can see the guards' barracks from here?" he said, standing up on his hind legs and smooshing his feline face to the window panes, his breath fogging the glass. "I bet Cassidy is in there right now having breakfast..."

It was probably for the best that he stayed behind, Ella reflected as she walked down the staircase after the diminutive Goldilocks. Tom had a terrible habit of not holding his tongue around strangers, and despite Ella's relationship with the queen, and her newfound role as tax collector, the fewer people who discovered she was harbouring a talking cat, the better. Magic was banned, after all. Gosh. What would

Harold do with such scandalous information if he were to uncover her secret? It didn't bear thinking about...

"Talk about fortunate timing," Goldi announced as they both heard Harold and Hillary's voices drifting up the staircase when they descended to the shared basement level that connected the town hall and post office a few minutes later.

Harold was complaining bitterly about Hillary embarrassing him in the meeting that morning in front of the queen.

"Someone might hand in the key I dropped," Hillary mumbled. "I'm really sorry, Dad. You can take the cost of a new key out of my wages."

"It's not the cost, it's the *principle*. The post office is a paragon of reliability and integrity!" Harold retorted as he breathed in deeply to fasten the last of his snug waistcoat buttons. "Two keys lost in one month! Disgraceful! This carelessness is exactly why you didn't get that promotion."

"But Dad, you said if—"

"No *buts*, the promotion is off the table. You will remain a junior clerk, as I told you last month..." He clamped up on realising Goldi approached with Ella in tow.

"Good morning again, Postmaster," Goldilocks chirped brightly, with the awkwardness of one having to pretend they had not overheard the pair's argument. "Sorry to bother you, but we need to access the old tenancy records in blueprint storage."

"If you *must*. Hillary will accompany you." Harold's lips curled in disgust, but Hillary looked genuinely relieved at the interruption to the berating she was receiving.

"Sure, but ah, Dad, sorry, I'll need the key back," Hillary apologised.

"Of all the!" Harold threw his hands up. "I just got this buttoned up again! Forget it, I'll take you myself. Hillary, come along. You can stay with them and make sure they don't go through any of the post office's private documents."

How rude! Ella thought. As if they would even want to look through the post office's *tedious* documents!

With no regard for protocol, or even *ladies first,* Harold clomped ahead down the narrow, darkened basement corridor, pausing only to adjust the gas lamps that lined the walls.

Ella shared a sympathetic eye roll with Hillary behind Harold's back. Poor girl. Imagine having such an intolerant bullying toad for a father. She leaned on her stick out of habit and gestured for the others to go ahead and trailed after them down the narrow corridor while running the palm of one hand across the ancient stone blocks.

The grey stone walls were pleasantly warm. Charmington township was situated on a thermal seam that provided hot water for all of the residents, and now that the town had been in the grip of eternal winter for the past two decades, the natural resources had really come into their own. Once the basement levels had been stifling and unpleasant in summer, but now the chance to venture into them was a welcome retreat from the cold and ice above.

Ella slowed as she realised that everyone ahead had stopped outside an unobtrusive oak door that looked much like the others.

"But, Dad, are you sure this is the storage room you want?" Hillary tugged at her father's shirt sleeve. "Don't you keep your, you know, personal records in here?"

"That's on the east corridor. Sixth South is non-essential building blueprints," Harold muttered off-handedly, drawing out his key on the long shiny brass chain from the waistcoat pocket.

Goodness, Ella frowned. Was that key a master key? Did the *one key* open *every* door? The post office and town hall shared their basement level too. That certainly was a poor security feature—no wonder Hillary had been scolded if she had lost such a master key. Anyone who found it could let themselves into the post office and the town hall. Perhaps Ella should ask Tom to hunt for the lost key out in the snow before some ne'er-do-well got their hands on it?

"Yes, but that side was flooded with the pipes bursting," Hillary was whispering furtively. "You made me move some of your stuff. Remember? Your *stuff*?"

Ella perked up. What was Hillary implying? Oh, magic preserve, was Harold, pillar of reliability and integrity, harbouring a few forbidden items of his own? How delightful! "What's the holdup?" she called loudly. "I have important tax matters and repairs to attend to, you know."

"And I have the queen's hair to set," Goldilocks muttered, tapping a toe in the dimly lit basement.

Whatever message Hillary had frantically been trying to inform her dad, he seemed to have finally taken the hint. Panic danced across his mature features. Key in the door lock, he waved Goldi back. "Just tell Hillary what you want, and she will fetch it. There's no need for us all to cram in like sardines."

"Whatever." Goldi yawned in the fug. "Bring out the deed to the haberdashery building in Northgate Square. Should be under H for haberdashery or T for twins."

"T for twins!" Harold burst out, horrified by Goldi's filing system, but nonetheless, he turned the key and all but yanked Hillary by her shirt collar, pushed her in through the doorway and slammed the stout door behind her.

Gracious. That was unnecessary. Whatever was he—

From behind the door, Hillary started to scream. "Help! Cassidy! Ace! They're dead! They're dead!" The door flung open, and she stumbled out into the corridor and collapsed in a sobbing heap in Ella's arms. Harold, attached to the door by his keychain, struggled to pull the key free from the lock while trying to peer inside.

Goldi pushed past him. Her screams echoed Hillary's a second later. "Help! Help! Murder! There's been a terrible murder!"

Stuck behind Harold, and with Hillary's near deadweight in her arms, Ella glanced inside at the darkened storeroom. She could see a set of map drawers, some boxes, and Goldilocks standing over someone clad in black leather sprawled on the floor.

"Who? Who's dead?" Ella questioned Hillary in her arms just as Tomcat suddenly reappeared, brushed past her boots, and darted into the room after Goldi.

Wild-eyed and hyperventilating, Hillary uttered, "Cassidy and Ace! They're both dead!" And then she fainted, swooning. Ella could not take the sudden weight and shrieked. Harold turned and caught his daughter, having ripped the chain from the lining of his waistcoat.

Freed from the burden of holding up Hillary, Ella elbowed past father and daughter and followed Tomcat into the storeroom just as Goldi ran out shouting, "Ace is dead! Killed by a murderous human! Cassidy has murdered Ace!"

CHAPTER 4

THE PLOT THICKENS

BLUEPRINT STORAGE, POST OFFICE BASEMENT.

Clutching her walking stick aloft like a sword, Ella entered the small, windowless storeroom. She tapped the stick twice sharply against the flagstones. The tapping automated the walking stick's additional mechanical features. A pool of light six feet wide spilt out to illuminate the cramped storage area. Ella crouched down beside the two bodies. The little craftsman Ace was pinned under Cassidy's taller, slim form.

"Ace! Cassidy!" Tomcat cried, his small cat body helpless to shift the fallen pair. "Ella, help me! I can't lift her, oh Cassidy! Please don't be dead!"

Cassidy was slumped across Ace as if she had been dumped there. Her black hair was matted with blood on the back of her head. More blood pooled on the floor. Gently, Ella rolled the young guardswoman off her colleague. Cassidy groaned as Ella moved her, and Cassidy's hands flexed, clutching a heavy brass candlestick to herself as if for protection.

Magic preserve! Ella felt a rush of relief. Cassidy was alive!

And Ace? Poor little Ace! Ella knelt across Cassidy's stricken form while Tomcat whimpered and gently combed back the hair tangled across her face. "Will she be okay? Ella? Will she?"

"Of course," Ella said stoically, whether she believed it or not. This was no time to panic. *Keep it together, old girl,* she told herself.

Ella placed her fingers on the craftsman's throat, but his skin was cold and lifeless. Dead. Ace's face was stained with black, all down his chin. His little brass and rose-coloured magical glasses were bent, and one lens was missing. Ella gently removed the spectacles and folded them away into her skirt pocket. She glanced around the room. How had the pair ended up here? Seeking an answer to her question, she tried to take in the surroundings, while out in the corridor, Goldi and Harold were in the middle of an odd shouting match.

"This is the last straw!" cried Goldi. "Another craftsman murdered by a human! I won't stand for it!"

"Whatever are you talking about, you odious little creature?" Harold snapped back. "Ace probably attacked her. They must have broken in here and fought over what they were stealing."

"Goldi!" Ella shouted. "Get in here, please. Cassidy's alive."

Ella scanned the interior. The room was small and basic, lined with shelves, and oddly enough, there was a comfy chair surrounded by stacks of old newspapers and discarded chocolate wrappers. Most of the space was dominated by a set of map drawers on which were piled account books or ledgers and a case of something...bottles of alcohol, Ella realised as she got to her feet and peered into the wooden crate marked Mossfern. Aha! This little nook must be Harold's secret drinking room. Not such a pillar of society after all...

"Goldi!" Ella shouted again. "I need your help!"

"Oh, *my* help, you need *my* help!" Goldi intoned incredulously from the doorway. "Too bad! Magic is banned! So murderous, bribe-taking *humans* can get help from a *human* doctor! Out of my way!" And she barged past Harold and stormed off down the corridor.

Tomcat looked up at Ella with big, wet green eyes. "Ella, please, tell me what I can do!"

"Last month, the Book Club ladies mentioned there was a doctor. Do you know where he lives?" Ella asked in a whisper, glancing towards the door, but Harold was shaking his daughter and yelling at her to wake up—he was paying her and Tom no attention.

Tomcat nodded. "Yes, there's a hospital on Hot Cockle Lane!"

"Good. Run there, fast as you can, fetch help. Try to be discreet—don't get yourself captured!"

Tomcat didn't wait for more instructions. He raced off in a flash of white fur.

Ella removed her cloak and folded it, and then placed the soft bundle under Cassidy's head. Cassidy moaned again, and Ella winced. After a slight struggle, she unclamped the guardswoman's vice-like grip from about the heavy brass candlestick. Goodness, could Goldi be right? Did Cassidy bludgeon Ace with this?

Ella squeezed Cassidy's hand. "Help is on the way, my dear. I just need to check on Hillary, but I'll be back in a moment." Cassidy didn't respond. Her eyes were closed, and her breathing was shallow.

Ella stepped out into the narrow corridor where Harold was cradling Hillary, who was only just coming around from her faint.

Why hadn't Goldi wanted to help Cassidy? It didn't make sense. Surely, she couldn't think Cassidy would hurt Ace, or vice versa? They were friends and colleagues. Weren't they?

"Do you have any idea what upset Goldilocks?" Ella asked Harold once she was certain Hillary had not injured herself when she fainted. "What was Goldi saying about bribes?"

Harold shrugged, his attention on his daughter. But then he looked up. "Oh! Yesterday, Ace and Cassidy had an argument. Ask anyone. It was a very public spat. Did you hear, Hillary? It was right outside the post office in the square."

Hillary, still very pale, got to her feet. "I think so... They were shouting about Ace *not* taking something...?"

Harold's eyes went wide. "Yes! I remember now. Ace said Cassidy could do what she wanted, but *he* didn't take bribes! And now look! He's dead, and Cassidy has killed him."

CHAPTER 5

THE ADAPTED HOSPITAL

The basement corridor quickly became overcrowded as staff from the town hall and post office ventured below to investigate all the shouting. Ella held onto Cassidy's hand but was forced to move out of the way as the new doctor was let through. An unusually tall and thin, bald man dressed in a black duster with a serious air and a strong odour of carbolic soap. He directed his attendants with precise instructions, and both Ace and Cassidy were swiftly loaded onto stretchers and carried away, with Tomcat following after them.

When Ella made it back out of the warren of basement corridors, she was frazzled and disorientated. Finding herself in the foyer of the main post office, she was relieved to be above ground once more. Usually, the post office was a building she avoided because of Harold's unwelcome presence.

She sought a moment to gather her wits on one of the many bench seats that lined the walls. She sat next to a small child with a blond bobbed haircut. The child was dressed in an eye-wateringly loud, canary-yellow velvet outfit of breeches and cut-away jacket, all festooned with lace collar and cuffs.

The child kicked at the bench seat in a bored fashion. "All right, missus?" they enquired, sitting up from their bleak slouch of gloom. Despite their luxurious, if lurid, clothing, the child gave off a distinct attitude befitting a street urchin.

"Have we met, dear?" Ella replied, dredging her memory. There was something familiar about the child, but she couldn't quite place them. She certainly would not have forgotten such an outfit!

"Name's Olly," said the child, offering a small grubby hand, which Ella dutifully took and shook most somberly.

Olly? Was that short for Olivia or Oliver? Their bobbed hairstyle was more commonly for a girl, but dressed as a boy, they could be either...not that it truly mattered.

"Good day to you, Olly. I am Good Mother Ella."

Olly grinned. "Know who you are. You're the cat lady."

Ella pressed her lips together. Cat lady, was she? Well, it could be worse—and would be once all of Charmington learned of her new role as the tax collector. She'd dream of being referred to as 'the cat lady' then, no doubt!

The child wiped a hand across their nose, and the motion triggered a memory. Last month, Tomcat had been playing with a bunch of orphan children dressed in matching blue and yellow striped jumpers. They had batted bars of soap, carved to resemble boats, back and forth across the ice of the frozen-over unicorn water fountain in the middle of Northgate Square. The children thought it was tremendous fun when a cat joined their game. And then later, when Millie accused her sister Sally of being infected with the werewolf virus, the children had helped when Sally fainted...

"Is your cat with you today?"

Where was Tom? A good question. Ella had lost track of him in the commotion. No doubt he had followed the stretcher-bearers all the way to the hospital, wherever that was. Hot Cockle Lane, Tom had said. Could that be right? Hot Cockle Lane was an industrial, working-class area, Ella recalled. Her late sister Cinderella had installed the Cinderella Charity Animal Sanctuary in a disused warehouse at the bottom of the lane, but there certainly hadn't been a hospital for Charmington's human residents at that time. Back then, when magic was allowed, there was a multitude of various medical clinics and spas dotted across the township; they had never required a large central hospital.

"I wanted to tell him, I is going to be adapted," Olly continued, gesturing to their bright velvet outfit. The child flicked the lace cravat spilling out at their throat. "Gonna be a proper toff an' all."

"Adapted?" Ella blinked, trying to follow the child's meaning. Idly, she placed a hand on the heavy chain of office about her throat; the sound of the chain links clinking was still a novelty. "Oh, *adopted*, I see. Congratulations."

"Can I look at your unicorn necklace? I ain't gonna steal it. Double Baker Street promise." Olly placed both hands to the side of their head in some odd form of salute.

"Well, one can hardly refuse a double promise," Ella commented and unhooked the heavy chain from about her neck, then handed it gently to the child.

"Feel the weight of this!" Olly whistled and inexplicably extracted a jeweller's loupe from a pocket, which they placed to an eye with practiced ease. "Craftsman construction, pre-Albion era, eighteen carats over lead. Nice, very nice." They handed the chain back. "You don't get copies better than that, missus."

"Beg pardon?" Ella uttered, more than a little surprised by the whole exchange, but the echo of footsteps distracted her, and she glanced up as someone in a hurry approached her resting spot. Dressed in coachman's livery, a purple frock coat, black wig and tricorn, it was Dirk Turpin, Sibylla's royal coachman—and Cassidy's uncle!

Ella leapt to her feet, anticipating Dirk's flood of questions. "Ma'am, people told me to come here. Rumour is Cassidy's been badly hurt? Do you know anything? Is it true?"

"The doctor has taken her to the hospital," Ella responded, clasping the coachman's hands in hers. "I don't know where the hospital is located. Do you?"

"Bottom o' Hot Cockle Lane," Olly piped up helpfully.

"Is that near the animal sanctuary?" Ella questioned.

"Same place," Olly returned with a shrug.

Magic preserve! That did not bode well.

Dirk removed his tricorn and clutched it to his chest. "Yes, of course, the hospital, right you are." The coachman was white as a sheet. "Oh lord, her poor mother, my sweet sister. I promised her I'd look out for Cass," Dirk mumbled to himself, anguish etched across his face. "Should never have encouraged her to join the watch. Dangerous work, sweet sister, forgive me!"

"Did you say Cassidy? The guard lady?" Olly tapped Ella's elbow, and she nodded, not wanting to distress the child or uncle with the grisly details.

"Let me accompany you," Ella suggested, squeezing Dirk's hands. "Whatever assistance I can offer is yours. Come along, this way, I won't slow you down."

"Right you are, much obliged, ma'am," Dirk uttered, repeatedly swallowing and wiping a sheen of sweat from his brow.

Ella nodded good day to young Olly and guided Dirk through the gawking citizens queuing to post their parcels. Poor chap, it was always horrifying to hear of a loved one being hurt and feeling helpless to do anything. "The sooner we get there, the sooner we can assure ourselves of Cassidy's well-being."

ELLA WAS NOT SURE WHAT she had been expecting to find. She had never been into a non-magical hospital, but she wouldn't have imagined anything this wretched. The former animal sanctuary, once divided into stabling and various pens for all manner of creatures, from lame horses and stray dogs and cats to injured birds, had been all swept away to form one open, rather gloomy space. Basic cots in orderly rows were laid out under the wide canopy of the old warehouse roof—a roof that had seen better days.

A few months ago, she had been raising money for the animal shelter—or thought she had. And where were the animals now?

Cooing pigeons sheltered in the rafters between the large exposed oak beams, and there were many gaps in the tiled shingles where daylight streamed through to illuminate random spots within the stark interior. Strategically placed buckets were positioned to collect the constant *drip, drip* of water, as ice and snow from the poorly maintained roof leaked into the dim space.

Nearly every bed was occupied, with very little thought given to privacy. A few beds had threadbare sheets hung like curtains around the cots, but most were open for all to see. Several braziers were lit and smoking slowly, so the room was not freezing cold, but surely, in the dead of night, this must be a horrid place.

Ella paused on the threshold, taken aback by the humble surroundings. Dirk's eyes adjusted quickly to the gloom, and he pointed, having spied Cassidy being attended to by the doctor across the far side of the wide space. Cassidy's hospital bed had the advantage of a direct beam of sunlight, and the doctor was in the final stages of wrapping gauze around her head.

Ella made her way more slowly after Dirk across the flagstone floor, her hobnail boots echoing painfully loudly with each step. She tried to creep and not disturb the patients, many of whom were sleeping, as the groans of people in discomfort and pain made her stomach clench. Oh, what a dreadful place! It had never occurred to her that without magic to heal them, *how* did the general population cope? What she saw laid out before her was positively barbaric.

Shocked, Ella stopped short before a cot where a familiar-faced woman was propped up, one leg awkwardly suspended and encased from ankle to thigh in plaster. The woman opened one eye, and Ella gasped upon recognising her—Nigella Pickford, a local actress.

"Are...are you all right, my dear?" Ella stuttered, abashed, when Nigella caught her staring.

Nigella cast an annoyed glance at her nearest neighbour, who was sprawled out on top of the sheets and snoring loudly, a short red cape pulled tightly around her tubby body. Ella gasped again. Marge the midwife! Had she, too, suffered a terrible injury?

"Would you mind?" Nigella rasped, hand to her throat and gesturing to the water pitcher on a small table beside her cot. It was just out of reach, incapacitated as she was. "I'm paying Marge to tend me while I'm stuck here," she uttered grievously, her full bosom swelling with indignation, as she tugged and tried to arrange the sheets to give her more comfort or dignity. "Money well spent, I think not!"

"She's not...hurt then, also?" Ella asked while pouring Nigella a glass of water, handing it to the actress and then setting the twisted sheets to rights.

"Ahh, thank you," Nigella breathed, gulped down the water, and then flung another narrow-eyed look full of daggers at the midwife. "Passed out *drunk*," Nigella hissed, but then added conversationally, "There was a large party at the new police station last night—Axel was handing out all the booze left over from the café's wine cellars. Quite the shindig, by Marge's intoxicated account."

"Oh, goodness," Ella muttered. Taking the empty glass, she refilled it and then moved the table closer so that Nigella might reach it herself when needed.

A few rows down, a book slammed closed. Ella glanced up to see over, in the shadows, what looked like a blonde girl with cute pigtails, wearing a denim dirndl and yellow duckie boots. She was perched at the bedside of a pallid-faced old man with wheezing, rattling breath.

Gretel. Ahh... She must be doing her infamous deathbed watch. Gretel often claimed she had many enemies, and her strategy in dealing with them, or so Ella had heard, was simply to outlive them. But there was also a common myth that one couldn't die when surrounded by enemies—and so people would pay Gretel to sit beside terminally ill relatives, hoping that it would gain them extra time.

Gretel peered at the man, asking, "Are you dead yet?" The old man feebly waved her off, and she glowered, flashing a set of little razor-sharp white fangs. "*Nein, nein*, is alvays *nein* with you..." She settled back in the shadows and flicked her book open, but then suddenly slammed it shut with a bang. "Aha! Did zat frighten you to death? *Nein*? Fine, zen we read one more chapter..."

"I don't suppose you have a copy of today's *Nottingham Times*?" Nigella asked hopefully. "I'm putting in an advert for upcoming auditions for the Christmas play, and I want to make sure that Spalding got the wording right."

"No, sorry," Ella said, "but I'll try to have one brought to you later." She turned away, but a beam of sunlight from a hole in the roof temporarily blinded her, and she bumped into the tall doctor, all dressed in black.

"Ahh, yes..." he voiced in a cool, measured tone laced with disapproval, eyes glancing at the golden insignia chain around her neck. "At long last, the rental inspector. Excellent. I have a few complaints to make to our landlord. There, there, and there!" He pointed to various holes in the roof. "The rent increases for maintenance and yet the roof is never repaired! What are you going to do about it?"

"Me?" Ella found herself on the back foot. Goodness, to think that she had been raising money for the animal sanctuary for years, selling her pumpkin soup at the weekly market—that was until young Tom April had come along two months ago and upended her life and halted all soup production. She hadn't realised the few coins she had made were going to gauze and roof tiles. Oh dear! "Umm, sorry, I actually just came to see..." She gestured towards Cassidy's bed.

The doctor crossed his arms and sighed, a look of tight disdain on his hawkish features as if this was exactly the typical pass-the-buck response he expected from a town official.

"Ah, perhaps you could give me a list of the things you need to be done...?" Ella suggested and patted her pockets. "I don't have a piece of paper on me, but I'm sure I'll remember."

"I'm sure you *won't*," cut off the doctor, and he stalked off, disappearing into what used to be the horse tack room, but now had "Doctor Hyde – Office" painted on the door.

Feeling horribly guilty, Ella ventured over to the cot Cassidy occupied. The young guardswoman's head was neatly bound, her eyes were open, and she was talking softly to her uncle Dirk perched on the edge of the bed. Tomcat was at the foot, sitting up straight as a soldier on guard duty overseeing a precious treasure.

Ella's heart twinged. Poor Tom, it was clear to her the boy was smitten with Cassidy, but trapped in cat form, it was unlikely he could win her heart. She shook the notion off as Dirk got to his feet and ushered her close.

"Ma'am, please sit here. The good doctor says we must keep Cass awake because o' the concussion."

"Oh yes, and you need me to talk to her. Certainly, I can do that," Ella replied and perched on the side of the cot, where the coachman had been.

"No, no, Dirk will stay and keep her awake," Tomcat spoke up like it was all decided. "We need you to help me solve Ace's murder and find out who attacked Cassidy!" His white tail flicked back and forth.

"Solve Ace's murder?" Ella gulped. The memory of the heavy brass candlestick Cassidy had been clutching darted through her mind. "I'm not sure—"

"No need for modesty, ma'am," Dirk replied, his face plastered with earnestness. "Tom explained how he solved Rum's murder, and then you helped him solve that werewolf thing just last month!"

"Oh, did he now?" Ella voiced tightly.

Tomcat ducked his small head, his ears dipping. "I know you warned me not to talk, but this is important!"

There was that, of course, but more than that, Ella remembered it the other way around! That Tom had *assisted* while *she* had solved those murders. Tom had definitely been off somewhere eating brownies when she had unveiled Arthur's killer!

"Please, ma'am," Dirk begged, placing a hand on her shoulder. "Everyone knows Sheriff Axel and Cass don't get along—he won't put any time into solving this case. But I know you and Mr. Tom can figure this out together. Please? I promised my sister I would look after Cass like my own daughter..."

Ella patted Dirk's hand. "Of course, I shall *assist*." She glanced at Tomcat, who had the good grace to look a little embarrassed, but really, she couldn't entirely blame him. Trying to impress the girl he loved. It was sweet.

Cassidy groaned, and it was Ella's turn to feel guilty. Really, it didn't matter who got the credit. Ace had been killed and Cassidy very nearly, as well. As Tom said, this was important.

"Cassidy, my dear," began Ella, "do you know who I am?"

Cassidy regarded her with dark eyes, and blinking slowly, she whispered, "Are you the cat lady?"

Ella sighed. "Quite so. Now tell me, what happened to you and Ace? What's the last thing you remember?"

CHAPTER 6

CUSHIONS AND ROOSTERS

CHARITY HOSPITAL, HOT COCKLE LANE, CHARMINGTON.

"What's the last thing you remember, dear?" Ella coaxed.

"Ace was on the ground... Something black on his face." Cassidy raised her hand to her mouth, and Ella recalled the black stains she had seen about the little craftsman's mouth.

"Where did you see him on the ground? Can you remember the location?"

"Not sure..." Cassidy writhed, anguish etching her face. "Underground." She spread her palms as if remembering the touch of something. "Dark space... Machinery. I could smell turpentine."

Tomcat hunched forward, little sharp claws digging into the thin cot mattress. "That's a good clue, Cass! Keep going."

Cassidy shut her eyes briefly. "Rooster...?" she whispered, but then shook her head as if the memory had escaped her.

Tomcat tensed at Ella's side as if he was going to interrupt again, but Ella held a finger up to halt him.

"How about last night in general?" Ella suggested after a minute of silence. "Do you remember what you did?"

"I...went to Axel's promotion party...?" Cassidy pressed the heel of her palm to her bandaged forehead. "Noisy... Lots of people. Rooster..." Cassidy repeated. She flinched and clutched her temples. Trying to sit up, she suddenly patted her ribcage as if searching for something. "At the party, I received a message. Ace had seen Rooster!"

Dirk swept off his tricorn and crouched beside the cot. "Rooster is a wanted criminal—a terrible thug!" he said, explaining for Ella's benefit. Little did the coachman know that last month Cassidy and Ace had filled Ella and Tom in on a smuggling ring they were trying to shut down and this one-eared Rooster chap was a prime suspect. Ella didn't recall all the details, except it was something to do with a special ink called Pendragon Green that was used for printing paper money in Avalon.

"But Rooster is in Nottingham prison," Tom whispered at Ella's elbow.

"He was due out," Ella amended, having been given this information by a very reliable source, Wulf, who was Prince John's bodyguard. Wulf had once been a prisoner in that very place, but now hunted down John's enemies, thanks to his unique abilities.

Cassidy was still patting her shirt front at her side. "Jacket? Where's my jacket? I have a hidden pocket…"

The black leather guard's jacket was looped over the top of the bed frame, and Ella took it up and found the little secret pocket on Cassidy's instructions.

"I would have stashed the message there," Cassidy whispered, lying back on the narrow cot.

Ella's fingers brushed against paper folded in a little tight square. "Oh! I have it! Oh, it's very valuable, I know it!" She unfolded the paper wad as Dirk and Tomcat leaned in close.

But it wasn't a message. Ella wasn't entirely sure what it was at first. But certainly, it was valuable, that much was obvious. She knew it in her bones. It was a rectangle of thick paper, with the words *Avalon Legal Tender One Dollar* printed in green. Other than that, it was partially ripped and had a rather large black splotch. "Ohh…this is that new-fangled paper money!"

Tomcat nodded. "There was an article in the *Nottingham Times*, wasn't there? Prince John wants to introduce paper banknotes like what they use in Avalon."

"Paper money?" Dirk muttered. "Foolish idea—how do you stop it from burning up? Gold may melt in a fire, but it's still usable after it cools down." He tutted. "I won't be asking to have my wages in paper, that's for sure."

Ella was inclined to agree. Paper for money! How ridiculous. Although, clearly, this banknote was valuable indeed. All her instincts said so. What an interesting development…

She offered the banknote to the injured guardswoman. "Is this what you were given?"

Cassidy shook her head. "I don't remember…" She shut her eyes and lay back as Dirk rifled through the outer pockets of the jacket.

"Sweet mercy!" he exclaimed, extracting a fistful of Avalon banknotes from the main side pocket. These ones were all printed with an ascribed value of one hundred dollars each.

"Are they just as valuable as this one?" Ella asked, still clutching the ripped banknote with the black splotch. She wasn't familiar with the value of Avalon currency, let alone paper money. It was all quite confusing.

"This is hundreds of dollars," Dirk hissed, fanning the notes out. "Cassidy, why do you have all this paper money?"

Oh dear, a dark thought popped into Ella's head. *Bribes.* While she wasn't sure how *'dollars'* stacked up in value against gold and silver, Harold had said Ace had accused Cassidy of taking bribes... "I will just hang onto this one for safekeeping, shall I?" Ella said, slipping the blotched banknote into her skirt pocket.

"What do I do with all these?" Dirk whispered, pushing the one-hundred-dollar banknotes under his niece's nose.

"Not mine," Cassidy murmured, feebly batting him away.

After sharing a pained look with the other two, Dirk stuffed the handful of Avalon banknotes into his tricorn and pulled it down tight over his head.

"What about the blotched one, Cass?" Tom asked. "That was in your hidden pocket."

Cassidy squeezed her eyes shut. She was very pale. "Don't remember. I must have picked them all up somewhere."

Ella glanced around the hospital room, but no one was paying their whispered conversation any heed. Those who weren't asleep were clearly wrapped up in their own pains and unlikely to be listening in. Across the far side of the warehouse, however, the tall doctor was standing, arms crossed in his office doorway, staring at them. His hawkish features expressed grave disapproval. Ella had the distinct feeling they were going to be kicked out very shortly. Perhaps they better wrap up their questions for now and come back later.

"Is there anything else you can add about Rooster?" she whispered the moment Doctor Hyde stalked back into his office. "Think back. You were at Axel's noisy party when someone gave you a note about Rooster. Shut your eyes. Can you see who approached you with the message?"

"Yes... Someone, someone dressed like a fancy cushion?" Cassidy sat up and winced, clutching her head. "Wait! Yes! It wasn't a written note, it was a *messenger,* it was the Baker Street orphan, Olly! I remember I was at the party, and Olly came up and told me that Ace had given them a message to tell me."

"I must insist this stops immediately!" Doctor Hyde snapped, suddenly looming over them. "I said to keep her awake with quiet conversation, not harass her mental capacities!"

"But—" Tomcat uttered just as Ella clamped her hand across his mouth. She pinned the little cat to her side and stood up.

"Quite so, Doctor Hyde. We must let the patient rest. I apologise. We'll be going," Ella said politely. "Perhaps you can tell me the list of repairs you need as we walk out?"

"Huh! I can do one better. A gift to mark the occasion of your appointment to town official," the tall doctor said coolly, holding out a rather fine leather-bound notebook with its own pencil. The notebook was opened to a fresh page, and at the top, in barely legible handwriting, was written: Top Priority – fix hospital roof.

"Thank you, most kind," Ella said, taking the notebook in her free hand while keeping Tomcat firmly tucked under her elbow. "Good day, Doctor. I will ensure that the hospital receives as much assistance as I can offer."

"Harrumph," muttered Doctor Hyde and spun on his heel. He began weaving up and down the shadowy rows, checking each patient, while overhead pigeons fluttered, and the constant *blip blip* of water fell with the regularity of ticking clocks.

"Good day, Cassidy. And Dirk, I will find someone to relieve you in a couple of hours..." Ella cast her gaze about the other wretches lying bed-bound while the lone doctor attended to each with his abrupt manner and terse efficiency. She slid out the pencil from the strap on the notebook and added: *more staff/nurses for the hospital* under Doctor Hyde's scrawl.

As they walked out between the rain buckets and beds, from the crook of her arm, Tomcat whispered, "Where to first?"

Ella placed the notebook and pencil in her skirt pocket. "First, we go talk to the fancy cushion."

"Huh?"

"Olly. We go find young Olly."

CHAPTER 7

ORPHAN OLLY

HOT COCKLE LANE, LOWER WEST SIDE, CHARMINGTON.

Once out in the street, the sharp, wintry chill cleansed her lungs of the fug of smoke and disinfectant odours that saturated the hospital. She hadn't been in Hot Cockle Lane for a long time. It had always been a bustling little street, filled with all manner of businesses, trades, and retailers, all crammed together, from the barrel maker to the man with the upturned barrel playing a fast game of *find the pea* to a rapt audience. But today, it seemed busier than Ella had ever encountered before.

Ella set Tomcat down to get her bearings and mentally navigate the quickest route to the Baker Street orphanage. Steam rose from the street vents, and the sound and scent of industry enveloped the whole area.

"What's the holdup?" Tomcat asked, jumping up onto a pile of wooden crates marked *"Lynn's Patented Fat-soap – smells like beef, scours like sandpaper,"* outside a barbershop.

"There used to be a shortcut to Baker Street I would like to take," Ella voiced, thinking back to years before. "I think it was between Betty's Pies and the Bright White Laundress…"

"Baker Street? No, we don't need to go to the orphanage. Olly is staying at the twins' haberdashery in Northgate Square."

"Is he indeed?" Ah, that certainly explained the sudden change in the style of young Olly's clothing from homely jumpers to fancy cushion. "How ever do you know all that?" Ella asked, tapping her walking stick against the ice-damp cobblestones as she strode along Hot Cockle Lane. "You haven't been talking to him, have you?"

"Olly is a them," Tomcat said, trotting to catch up. "Not a him."

"Beg pardon?" Ella asked, glancing down at the prancing cat, and then waiting to cross the street as a donkey wagon laden with sacks of potatoes turned the corner.

"It's simple, really," Tom explained at Ella's feet. "Olly doesn't choose to be identified by their gender—whatever *you assume* that to be. So, you refer to Olly as them, not him or her."

Ella pinched the bridge of her nose. "Not him or her..." Comprehension struck at last. "Ohh, I see, now I'm with you. Neither one nor the other, like a dragon, you mean. Fine, now I understand. You should have said Olly is like a dragon."

"Dragons are non-binary?"

"Certainly, or they were. I thought everyone knew that? Look it up in Merlin's *Guide*. It's all there in black and white, or should I say grey?"

She stood aside to let a man carrying a large coil of rope over his shoulder go past.

The man doffed his cap to her with a raspy, "Mornin', Good Mother." Followed by a chuckle and a wink at Tom along with, "Mornin', Tom. Caught any rats today?"

Tomcat pressed his little front paws together and ducked his head as if expecting a scolding.

Ella just sighed. "Tom, is there anyone left in this town who *doesn't* know you can talk?"

Not wanting to hear the answer, she didn't wait for his reply and walked on.

Really! The lad had no common sense at all. Magic was banned on pain of death! He was a talking cat! Axel had already made it very clear that she could expect no clemency from him.

She crossed under the archway between Castle Alley and into West Avenue, and a minute later they were back in Northgate Square, standing before the front of Mercer and Mercer, more commonly known as the twins' haberdashery.

Oh dear, something was definitely wrong between the twins, Ella thought as she glanced through the large front window that was normally filled with colourful displays of bonnets and ribbons. Instead of the usual display, newspapers had been plastered over the panes of glass, and a man on a stepladder was currently in the process of wrapping a length of calico fabric around the wooden sign hanging above the front door.

"Morning, Tom. How're the mice treating you?" the man called cheerily.

"You know, Cole, same old, same old."

Ella placed her hands on her hips and let out a deep sigh. The man, Cole, suddenly bobbed his head and touched a finger to his lips. "Oh right, mum's the word. No talking cats here," he said loudly over his shoulder in the direction of the former Gatehouse Inn, now the police station.

"Shall we try around the back?" Tom asked quietly.

"Yes, why don't we?" Ella followed Tom as he padded down the alleyway between the abandoned cluckoo shop and the twins' haberdashery.

Ella climbed the steps of the back porch, experiencing a moment of *déjà vu* as she regarded the railing where Willow's little poodle Mr. Puddles had been tied last month when she attended a book club meeting here. She knocked on the door, which was opened a second later by an elderly lady dressed in the canary-yellow pelisse coat she had been wearing just that morning during the council meeting.

Ah, Sally. At least the twins' disagreement meant it was much easier to tell them apart, as they weren't wearing identical outfits. "Good morning, Sally," Ella said as the old lady bobbed a curtsey.

"Good morning again, Lady Ella! How lovely to see you so soon," Sally burbled before Ella could get another word out. "You must be here to inquire about the next Book Club meeting—I'm so sorry to inform you we'll have to miss this month as we're undergoing some renovations."

"Oh, that's disappointing. Book Club was very entertaining last month," Ella said, which was at least half true. "Actually, I was hoping to speak to Olly. Might I have your permission to speak to your young ward?" Ella took a moment to run her words back through her head. Had she used any inappropriate pronouns?

Sally's cheerful smile faltered momentarily. "Why, of course, come in, come in." She guided Ella and Tomcat inside the lavender-scented backrooms to the cutting table. "I'm sure *Olivia* would be happy to assist you in whatever way *she* can. *Olivia!*" Sally shouted over her shoulder and then shared a rather strained smile with Ella when a sulky "Wot?" was yelled back.

"Won't you take a seat at the table? Please excuse the mess. I'll be back in a moment," Sally said between clenched teeth and a tight, fixed smile. She darted off down a hall, and there were a series of door slams.

Oh dear. Clearly, it wasn't all smooth sailing on the 'adaption' front. *Keep out of it, old girl*, Ella told herself. *None of your business.*

Ella pulled out a chair for herself and one for Tom as the large cutting table was absolutely covered in a higgledy-piggledy pile of ribbons, hat trims, hat boxes, and all manner of silk flowers, as if someone had scooped up armfuls and dumped them there.

Footsteps stamped down the hallway along with accusations of, "You agreed to call me Olly if I wore this itchy—"

"I agreed to call you Olly in private, but in public, we maintain appearances!"

"Don't say a word," Ella hissed a warning to Tom. "It's none of your business."

"But—"

"None!" Ella interjected, just as Sally appeared with young Olly in tow, looking very much as Cassidy described, a fancy cushion of yellow velvet and lace.

"See, Olivia, you have lovely visitors come all this way to see you!" Sally chirped, pushing Olly into the room.

Olly's eyes went wide on seeing Ella and Tom sitting there. "I ain't a snitch!" they cried, attempting to backpedal into the hallway, but Sally had been expecting it and blocked their path.

"Olly," Ella began, hoping that the use of their chosen name might show solidarity, "you're not in any trouble."

"I heard that before!" Olly protested, crossing their little arms, bottom lip jutting out in mimicry of the lace spilling out under their throat. "I know a stitch-up when I sees it."

Poor child, Ella sympathised. The outfit did look terribly itchy. She pushed the thought aside. Ace and Cassidy's situation was the most critical. "Sally, do you think we might have a word with your young ward alone? If that is all right with both you and the child?"

"We?" Sally replied rather wide-eyed, and Ella realised with a jolt that Sally had interpreted "we" as the royal we, not Tom and me, which was what she meant.

Guiltily, Ella touched the official chain about her neck, which only added to Sally's misinterpretation of the situation.

Sally bowed low, "Certainly, Your *Highness*." She made a wee squeak like she had been given some singular honour and gathered up her butterscotch clutch purse. "Why don't I go fetch some of those cream puffs you like, *Olly*? And you stay here and answer whatever questions Her *Highness* would like to ask."

Not waiting for Olly's response, Sally flourished a bow, much like Harold had that morning in front of Sibylla.

Ugh. It had taken years to train the older citizens to drop the use of her title, and now one tiny slip-up and Sally was all over it.

"And no swearing!" Sally hissed an aside at her ward before closing the door.

"Why didn't you tell me you're a 'Highness'?" Tom asked, his little cat head tilting left then right.

"Excuse me?" Ella blurted. "You do know the queen is my sister?"

Tomcat shrugged. "I guess I didn't think about it. You're just so ordinary."

"Thank you very much," Ella said tightly, before giving Olly what she hoped they would interpret as a friendly, open smile. "Now to the less ordinary business of the day. Please, tell us what happened last night. What's the message you gave to Cassidy? And who told you to deliver it?"

CHAPTER 8

THE MESSAGE

Olly arched an eyebrow and went and gave Tomcat a pat. "I said before, I ain't a snitch. I don't care if you're the queen of cats."

Magic preserve. This one was a tough customer. "How about we make a trade? I give you something you want, and you answer my questions about Ace and Cassidy."

"I'm listening," said Olly, leaning an elbow against the cutting table. "What you got? Gems and stuff?"

Ella rolled her eyes. "I was thinking, how about I get Sally to call you Olly in public, and maybe do something about the itchy lace?"

"You can do that?" Olly said with a low whistle. They hitched a thumb while addressing Tom. "Gov'nor, she got that much power? Or is she pulling my leg?"

Tomcat's whiskers fanned. "That much power and more!"

Olly narrowed their eyes. "All right, Gov'nor, you got a deal." They offered their recently scrubbed-clean hand to Tom, and the pair shook hand and paw.

"Why does Tom get the handshake?" Ella enquired, surprised.

Tomcat sat back on his haunches and crossed his furry arms across his little round stomach. "You heard Olly, I'm the governor."

"Exactly," Olly added. "Plenty of queens and kings. Only ever seen one talking cat."

"Fine," Ella said, unable to suppress an eye roll. Goodness. Outranked by a cat! That was a lesson in humility, not that she needed it. "Now, please, tell us everything you can remember about Ace and Cassidy from when you last saw them…"

Olly shook their head. "Nuh-uh. Ain't born yesterday. You gotta make a royal decree, see?" They tapped the lace-littered tabletop. "You writes down my demands, and then Missus Sally has to do it. And you gotta stamp it with the unicorn thing, so it's official." They gestured to the Unicorn seal on the chain of office about Ella's neck.

"Can you read?" Ella enquired, fetching out the notebook the terse doctor had given her and flipping it open to a fresh page.

Olly's bottom lip jutted again. "I can read lots of words." They started ticking off a list of common road signs. "West Avenue, donkey parking Fridays only, no hats, wait here for next teller, mind the step..."

Ella set to the task of fashioning a 'royal decree' on the clean sheet of notepaper, while Olly carried on demonstrating their reading prowess.

"Two-for-one beer at happy hour, fat soap, Betty's Pies, Gatehouse Inn, open, closed, cluckoo repair and polish, one dollar, *Nottingham Times*, please ring bell..."

"Ohh, and make your handwriting all swirly with lots of flourishes," Tomcat said, crowding close.

"Yeah! That too an' all," young Olly enthused, peering over Ella to see what she had written so far, which was:

To whom it may concern, by royal decree of Her Right Royal Highness, Ella Discretion Fortitude Gertrude Charming of Wyld Kingdom...

"Gertrude?" Tom snickered, little white whispers twitching. "Your middle name is Gertrude?"

Ella held her tongue and just turned to young Olly. "And your demands are?"

After a little negotiation, they finished the document with:

From this day forth, Olivia May shall be referred to as Olly May, and will be addressed as they or them, by all who do not want to be punished with death or spiders in their shoes. And every Sunday, there will be cream cakes or waffles, forever and ever.

The lack of ink or wax to stamp the seal with was overcome by Olly's suggestion that Sally's cranberry jam stained everything it touched.

Ella ripped the sheet out of the notebook and handed it to Olly. The child practically vibrated with happiness, holding the decree aloft and admiring the red jammy sheen of the royal unicorn crest against the crisp white paper.

"Now, about last night..." Ella prompted.

Olly set the decree down gently and, avoiding Ella's eye, examined their fingernails. "You can't tell Missus Sally. I wasn't meant to be out of bed, see?"

"Double Cat Lady promise," Ella said, crossing both sets of indexing fingers and touching her ear lobes.

Suitably placated, Olly scrunched their face, eyes darting to the ceiling as if thinking back. "Missus Sally wouldn't let me go to the sheriff's party." Olly hitched a thumb in the general direction of the new police station.

"I should hope not!" Ella uttered before she could stop herself.

Olly wrapped their arms defensively around their velvet-covered body and mumbled something about missing out on the opportunity to pick a lot of pockets, before tugging the hem of their velvet jacket straight. "So anyways, I snuck out on the back porch later. You know, to sit and watch, 'cos people use the back street behind the post office as a shortcut all the time, and sometimes drunk people drop stuff, and that's fair game then. That technically ain't stealing."

"Go on," Ella encouraged, sitting back.

"And Mr. Ace was outside in the alley between us and the old cluckoo shop. He were peering into the basement grate window. And there were a light on in there."

Ella and Tom sat forward. The cluckoo shop had been abandoned these past two months as Axel had forced the tenants out for not paying their rent.

"He keeps walking back and forth, you know, all upset like he can't make up his mind. And anyways, he sees me peeking over the railing at him—because yellow ain't stealthy at all. I asked for black velvet! Can I get that added to the decree?"

"Yellow is very becoming. You look like you're made of gold," Ella said quickly. "Go on, then what?"

Olly regarded their yellow sleeves for a second as if contemplating this 'gold' notion. "Anyways, he says, 'Do you know who Cassidy is?'" Olly rolled their eyes. "And I says 'course! Not born yesterday! Plus, she nabbed me stealing—*borrowing*—one of Betty's pies last month. And he says something about her being over at the big party, and can I give her an urgent message?" Olly crossed their arms and took a breath.

Tom tapped a paw on the back of Ella's hand. "Maybe you should take notes?"

"I was about to," she fibbed, flipping the leather notebook open again. "Please go on, my dear."

"And I said I'm not allowed to go to the party. And he says this is a special exception and he will come round tomorrow and give me a medal and a puppy—which was a lie, 'cos he still ain't showed up, and it's nearly nine." Olly huffed and kicked the floorboards.

Ella and Tom shared a tight look. There was a reason Ace had not followed through on his slightly dubious promise.

"And did you go?"

"O' course." The child shrugged. "I went and found Miss Cassidy and gave her the message. Easy as pie." Olly picked at their fingernails. "People saying this morning that she been nearly killed. That ain't true, is it?"

Ella pressed her lips together. She did not want to alarm the child with any gory details. "Cassidy is going to be fine. And your tale of what you heard last night will speed her recovery. What was Ace's message?"

Tom and Ella perched on the edge of their seats.

"Oh, that," Olly said, like it was old, boring news. "Rooster is in the cluckoo shop."

CHAPTER 9

THE CLUCKOO SHOP CLUE

TWINS' HABERDASHERY, NORTHGATE SQUARE, CHARMINGTON.

Tom pawed at the notebook sitting open on Ella's lap. "Write that down, write that down."

"I was going to," Ella said, this time not fibbing and jotting Ace's message down. "Rooster...is in...the cluckoo...shop. Thank you, Olly, you've been very helpful."

Olly twirled about on one foot and then picked up the decree. "Can't wait to show this to Sam and Sandy."

"Speaking of showing," Ella said, tucking the notebook away and smoothing her skirts as she stood up from the cutting table. "Can you please show us which window had the light on next door?"

"Sure," Olly said with a skip. "I'll just put this in my room first." They darted off down the hallway, clutching the sticky decree tightly.

Tomcat flicked his tail. "What are you planning on doing?"

"Isn't it obvious? I want to go investigate inside the cluckoo shop."

Tomcat's fur bristled, and his hackles stood up. "That's a terrible idea. With this dangerous Rooster character on the loose! He could be hiding in there. We should go report this to Axel. He's the sheriff."

Ella pulled a face and was about to retort when Olly returned, and they all ventured out onto the back porch in the cold morning air. Olly leaned over the railing and pointed to a small arched basement window set at ground level in the neighbouring building.

"Thank you, my dear..."

"Oh goodness, I'm pleased you're still here," exclaimed Sally, slightly breathless and trekking up the wooden flight of steps, bearing aloft a large cardboard box from Willow's bakery.

"We're just off," Ella explained, planting a hand on Olly's shoulder. "*Olly* has been very helpful indeed. *We* can only credit your good influence and compassion for *their* well-being. *We* are most moved," Ella added, throwing in a couple of positively royal *wes* for effect and let the chain of office run through her fingertips. "*Olly* is exactly the kind of youngster one hopes to see more of. We recall how gallant *they* were in coming to your aid during the werewolf incident."

"Oh, yes, that's true she—*they*—did come to my rescue." Sally blushed and curtseyed at least three times after passing the pastry box to Olly, who carried it inside straight away while licking their lips. Ella suspected the cutting room table was about to get a whole lot stickier.

Tomcat tugged on Ella's skirt, pointed a paw at the neighbouring building, and then placed his paw above his head. What was that about? Was the paw on the head meant to represent a pointy hat? A shark fin?

"All the best for your new...pet fish shop? Er, top hat business?"

But Tom kept pointing to his head and making a paw flick. Oh! He was trying to mime a cockerel crest. Of course, that made more sense. "What I mean to say is," Ella amended, taking Sally's gloved hands in her own, "do lock up tight tonight. I'm afraid there are reports of some rather nasty people about."

"Oh!" Sally's eyes went wide. "I heard about the attack on the watch members when I was in Willow's bakery." She gestured to the gas lamp posts lining the side street. "The gaslights went out last night! Do you think it could be connected?" Whispering in a conspiratorial fashion, she hissed, "I read a book where bank robbers doused the street lamps so they could tunnel unobserved into the bank!"

Ella leaned back a little and walked to the opposite side of the porch where Sally had indicated the side street. "Really? The whole row was out?"

Sally joined her at the railing, and Tomcat stuck his head through the slats and looked up and down the side street that ran the back length of the post office, haberdashery, cluckoo shop, and the bank.

"Well, from the post office at the far end, halfway down to here at least." Sally gestured past her property to the bank at the far end. "The bank's side stayed on, I think. Mostly I noticed the light outside my bedroom window was out, because when I got up in the middle of the night to, you know... Anyway, it was very dark, and I stubbed my toe something frightful."

"Hmm," Ella hummed thoughtfully. Was that a clue or merely a timely malfunction? Cassidy and Ace found in the shared basement of the post office and town hall, and a notorious criminal seen in the basement of a nearby abandoned building? Was it possible that the cluckoo shop basement *connected* to the basement of the town hall buildings? There certainly would be valuable items in those buildings. The takings from the post office, perhaps? Did they make a lot of money? Were stamps expensive?

And yet, when Ella had last spoken with Ace and Cassidy a month ago, they had thought Rooster was involved with smugglers. Still, thieves and smugglers must be cut from the same cloth. Why shouldn't a dyed-in-the-wool smuggler seize the opportunity to steal if the moment presented itself?

More than anything right now, Ella wanted to take a nosey in the cluckoo shop's basement.

"Perhaps you would be so good as to mention the gas outage to Mr....?"

"Mr. Beau," Sally prompted. "He has the tender for maintaining the gas street lamps."

Ella nodded brightly. She had thought Mr. Beau was the shoeshine man, but that didn't mean he couldn't manage the lamps as well.

Sally touched Ella's elbow and sighed. "I was just thinking of the old days. Do you remember? When every street was hung with all the little fairy lights?" She sighed longingly again. "It was so pretty back then. None of this smelly and unreliable gas, with the pipes thumping at odd times of the night."

"The lights thump?" Ella frowned. "That must make it hard to sleep."

Sally shrugged. "Not the lamps as such, some of the underground pipes connecting them, I always assumed. It had been quieter these past few years, but there was a frightful banging the last couple of nights." She tutted. "Nothing stays the same, does it? There's progress for you." Casting a wistful glance at her business and bidding Ella a good day, she ventured back inside the haberdashery.

"What were all the shark fin charades about?" Ella asked as she walked down from the porch to street level. She gripped the railing out of habit. Now that her knees were pain free, she was entirely steady on her feet.

"Proving to you I *can* keep quiet," Tomcat huffed and pantomimed the rooster crest flick again. "How could you ever think this was a shark fin? Are there any sharks around here? Hey, where are you going? Don't peer in there!" Tomcat scolded as she ventured over to the neighbouring building and crouched beside the basement window Olly had indicated. "What if Rooster is in there looking up and memorising your face?"

Ella stood up straight and dusted her hands. "Good luck to him. It's pitch black down there. If he were looking out at that very moment, I expect he only saw me as a silhouette." She looked up and down the alley and, seeing there was no one else about, headed for the empty shop's back door.

"Wait! What are you doing?" Tomcat hurried after her. "We should go tell Axel—don't touch that doorknob, I forbid it! I know you can somehow unlock locked doors!"

"Lawks! What nonsense are you spouting?" Ella said, turning the brass handle and feeling the lock give way. "Oh my! It is unlocked. How peculiar and most unexpected! Well, now it's my civic duty to investigate. Can't be helped..." She stepped inside and pulled the door closed just as Tomcat squeezed through in a rush of white fur, his hackles vibrating.

Stomping his little paws like he was marching on the spot, Tomcat hissed in the darkened back room, "I don't know how you keep on doing that, but you are going to tell me right now! Or else I'm going straight to Axel!"

"I'm fairly sure that would end up being worse for you than me..." Ella muttered while squinting into the dark. *Magic preserve!* The low light was something she hadn't considered. Her knees were behaving for once, but her eyesight was no better. She was going to have to use the walking stick's light, but should any villains be lurking in the basement, a lantern would definitely give away her advantage of surprise. "How's your eyesight in here?" she asked casually.

"I can see perfectly well, thank you, but—*aha!* You can't, can you?"

"Why don't you nip downstairs and scout around?"

Tomcat sat back on his haunches. "Nope."

Ella sighed. An impasse. At last, she said, "It's called the Keys to the Kingdom..." She gestured to the back door, which she knew had relocked after them. "My gift, with the locks, you see. It's a Charming family thing. We can all do it."

Tomcat's pink mouth fell open. "Wait, what? But that's magic! You said your magic was all bound up and you couldn't use it."

"This is Wyld magic, a family trait that has nothing to do with the magical powers I earned through my study into becoming a fairy godmother. *Those* powers are bound. I can't control the Keys to the Kingdom gift any more than Sibylla can stop this eternal winter that endures while she's queen. It's part of who we are."

"Wow!" Tomcat's pupils were as wide as his gaping mouth. "And you can magically unlock any door in the whole world?"

"Any *lock*, excluding bolts, but not the whole world, just Wyld Kingdom." She shrugged. "Not many people alive today remember, but it used to be kind of a thing. The Charming children, when presented at court, would prove their birthright, as it were, by opening a few locks. It always impressed dignitaries from other countries. Silly, really. I often wonder if it was the Keys to the Kingdom ability that gave Merlin his idea to help Arthur prove his birthright with the sword in the stone thing."

Tomcat shook his head in disbelief. "Can you imagine if you *could* open any lock in the entire world?"

Ella smiled thinly. "Yes, actually, that's one of the reasons we let the whole tradition of presenting the gift die down. People started to think exactly the same. Nasty people with nasty agendas. It got a bit dicey being a Charming for a time..." She gestured into the dark. "So, what do you say? Scout the place for me?"

"All right," grumbled Tomcat, adding, "Wait here," before he padded off to the narrow staircase that went down into the cluckoo shop's basement.

CHAPTER 10

WHAT THEY FOUND IN THE BASEMENT

ABANDONED CLUCKOO SHOP, NORTHGATE SQUARE, CHARMINGTON.

Ella had been leaning on her walking stick, running the events of the morning through her head for less than a few minutes, when Tomcat came zooming back up the stairs.

"Are you being chased?" Ella gasped, reaching for the back door handle in alarm.

"No, no, the basement is empty, but I found something! I found a clue!" He danced from one paw to the other, and Ella let out a relieved breath.

"Congratulations, your first clue—"

"Not my first. I've found plenty," grumbled Tom.

"If you say so," Ella replied. She tapped the walking stick twice against the floorboards, and the bright pool of light spilt out to guide the way. "Lead on." And she followed him down the narrow confines of the staircase into the warm depths of a large basement. It was divided into several interconnected storage rooms that ran along the length of the building. Ella counted the arched windows set at ground level as she walked. The window Olly had indicated was third along. As Ella walked, her hobnail boots rang out hollowly against the floorboards, and she stopped as a realisation struck.

"This is a wooden floor—not typical of a basement, which is more often dirt or flagstones." She met Tom's green eyes in the half-light. "There's a second basement!"

"That's the clue!" He nodded gleefully and darted over to a trapdoor half visible under a rug that Tom must have pulled back. The room was otherwise empty apart from a few tea crates and glass bottles. Tomcat pressed a pointed white and pink feline ear to the trapdoor. "There's no noise below. I'm nearly certain there's no one down there. Nothing big, anyway; a few mice, perhaps not even that."

Ella grimaced. The lock held no problems, but lifting the trapdoor itself might prove difficult if it was heavy or the hinges were poorly oiled.

Tom seemed to interpret her hesitation and said, "I could go fetch Cole, who was on the stepladder outside the haberdashery?"

Ella shook her head tightly. "Let me try first before we risk anyone else's life."

Tomcat's ears flattened to his head. "Cass will be okay, won't she? The doctor said head injuries are unpredictable, and I keep thinking maybe I should go beg Goldilocks to use her magic on the wound?"

"I have known Goldi for decades. Once she's made up her mind, there's no changing it without a solid reason. The quicker we prove both Cassidy and Ace were victims of the same rogue, the quicker we will have Goldi's help. Stand aside, I'm going to lift this on three, and it might slam back." Ella crouched, one knee down, one up, to get better leverage, and she slid the walking stick through the pull ring on the trapdoor. "One...two...three!" Ella heaved with all her might, her thin arms braced around the walking stick, using it as a lever to pull the trapdoor open. But the trapdoor shifted with surprising ease—a clever hinge on the underside engaged at the same time, and the door lifted smoothly and freely to reveal a ladder beneath.

A gust of warm air wafted up, laced heavily with paint or turpentine.

"You smell that?"

Tomcat nodded, surely recalling as Ella did what Cassidy had said. Turpentine. Cassidy had found Ace somewhere that smelled of turpentine. "Another clue."

Tomcat was about to leap into the darkened depths, but Ella called to wait and pointed the walking stick's light through the door. They both leaned over the edge and peered into the large room below. It was littered with paper, cans of something, paint or turpentine, and dominated by a large, black printing press.

"The source of the thumping that Sally heard, perhaps?"

Ella ventured down slowly, clutching the walking stick awkwardly. "What an inconvenient place to have a printing press!" Clearly, this was some covert operation. Stepping off the last ladder rung, Ella's boot crunched on glass. "Wait!" Ella warned, sweeping the stick light across the floor. Dark glass from a tall bottle or something was spread across the flagstone floor, fanning out from a large green stain.

A green stain! Ahh, just like on Axel's boots!

"Watch where you step. There's broken glass," Ella warned as Tomcat crept down the ladder and she toed the bottle fragments aside. As she did so, the light winked off something pink wedged in between two flagstones. She crouched down and gently eased the pink oval from where it was lodged.

Holding up the pink glass, Ella had a sense of *déjà vu*. "Does this seem familiar to you?"

"Not really," said Tom, and he leapt from the ladder straight up onto the giant old printing press. He pointed up. "Look!" Tom gestured to a row of glass globes hanging from the floorboards above the press. "Are those gaslights? Can't be, though, they're on strings…" He glanced down at the cans marked *Iron Drake Turpentine* beside the press. "Shouldn't have gaslights near all the turps either."

"Oh, my!" Ella realised what she was seeing. "Mechanical lights! They're a bit like fairy lights that have been enhanced with craftsman mechanicals…" She scanned the walls until she located a brass fitting. Then she turned the key in the fitting and the glass globes sprang to life, spilling out light and a faint humming noise. The whole room lit up. "I haven't seen mechanical lights in a domestic building for decades. They were very expensive and tricky to make."

Ella glanced down and noticed the little pink oval in her palm was all but aglow. "Magic preserve me!" Whether from memory or instinct, she held the oval up to her eye and surveyed the room. Nearly every surface glowed. The experience struck her as similar to when last month Ace had demonstrated the power of his rose spectacles to reveal Tom's embodied magical essence. She swung the pink oval towards him and squinted through it. Within Tomcat's body, a swirling mass of pink and purple lights glowed, and several light trails wound off his body like long leads snaking back up the trapdoor. "All the way back to the pumpkin patch…" Where Tom's human body lay in stasis within a giant pumpkin in her cottage garden.

Oh dear. This wasn't similar to Ace's magic-detecting spectacle lens. This *was* Ace's lens! Ella felt around in her pocket and drew out the bent pair of spectacles she had removed from the little craftsman earlier that morning.

She slipped the pink oval found on the floor into the spectacle frame. A perfect fit. She had expected no less.

"Ella," said Tomcat softly, peering over the far side of the printing press.

Black was splattered all over the flagstones in that corner of the room behind the press.

Ella held the rose spectacles to her eyes again. Through the lens, the black stains on the floor glowed intensely crimson, bright as the sun. Yanking the glasses away, she shut her eyes and blinked furiously, but she saw spots for several seconds.

"This basement must be the place that Cassidy described." Tomcat sat back on his haunches. "She and Ace must have interrupted Rooster up to no good."

"Certainly, it could be they interrupted *someone*," Ella said thoughtfully, looking back at the green stain at the bottom of the ladder, while also recalling the green under Axel's boots. Coincidence? Maybe, maybe not...

"We should go tell Axel what we found," Tom said, hitching a thumb up towards the trapdoor.

Hmm, if indeed Axel had also been down in here—Axel, who had a well-known grudge against Cassidy—and the green stain at the foot of the ladder was the source of the stain on his boots, then telling him of their discovery was probably not a good idea. She kept these thoughts to herself. If Tom thought Axel was involved, he would charge off immediately to attempt a citizen's arrest and get himself captured, or worse.

"What are you thinking?" Tomcat's pupil-dark eyes narrowed suspiciously.

"I'm wondering what they were printing," Ella fibbed, stooping to investigate the discarded balls of paper littering the base of the press. They were smeared with green as if used to wipe up a spill, or perhaps wipe down the press. On opening a scrunched paper ball, Ella had a jolt from the past.

"Oh, look at this, an old front page of the *Charmington Chatter!*" She spread it out before Tom up on his perch. He didn't seem inclined to prowl around on the floor, and Ella thought that best. Ink, glass, and spilt magic of some kind were hardly hygienic.

"Huh? It's some old newspaper...?" His white paw tapped a printed date. "This is from nearly sixty years ago!"

"Gosh, I had forgotten all about the *Charmington Chatter!*" Ella exclaimed, trying to read the paper's obscured headlines beneath the green smears. "Look, 'The Curse of the Scottish Play?' I remember that night! The annual midsummer ball. There was this hilarious incident when..." She caught Tom staring, and his tail was flicking. "Quite right, we're on an important mission. Time for reminiscence about stuffy dignitaries falling in donkey manure later."

She turned away from the press and went to investigate the neatly bundled stacks of paper on the far side of the space. They, too, were all old yellowing copies of the *Charmington Chatter* bearing that same headline. "Come to think of it, I have a feeling the *Chatter* was shut down about that time. There was a diplomatic incident following the manure. Princes don't like being called Prince-poo-shoes..." She bent down and gathered up a clean copy of the paper from the stack. "Might be fun to read this later."

In the meantime, Tom walked up and down the large press, smooshed his face into the crevices, and tentatively pulled a few levers. "You know what's missing?"

Ella shrugged, sliding the old *Chatter* edition into her deep skirt pocket.

"There's no printing plates!" Tom said rather triumphantly.

"Ahh, now that does sound like a clue," Ella concurred and joined Tom in peering furiously at the press machinery itself. She glanced down at the cans of turpentine. "I guess the plates get filthy and sticky, and so they are wiped with the turps... Maybe they have to take the plates away to be cleaned properly so they don't gunk up with dried ink?"

"Or maybe they don't want anyone to see the plates!" Tomcat beamed. "Surely, they aren't printing newspapers on this any more!"

"A good point..." Ella agreed. "I wonder what they're printing...?"

Tomcat's whiskers fanned in a smug halo. "Haven't you worked it out? I have!"

Ella crossed her arms and huffed. "Have you now? What, then, Mr. Smartycat?"

His feline grin stretched right across his face. "Money!"

CHAPTER II

WHO IS UP TO NO GOOD?

BASEMENT OF THE ABANDONED CLUCKOO SHOP.

"Paper money!" Tomcat repeated and swatted his little paw at the general area. "It makes sense. Remember last month Ace told us how they had found vials of the special Avalon money-printing ink called Pendragon *Green!*" He nodded enthusiastically, pointing to the green ink smeared across the old *Chatter* front page. "And don't forget all those one-hundred-dollar banknotes stuffed in Cassidy's pockets! She must have found them here and picked them up for evidence!"

"Evidence..." Ella muttered. Tom had a point. It certainly made sense. But why print Avalon currency? If some local criminals were going to counterfeit money, why not forge the banknotes that Nottingham was planning on adopting? Avalon currency wasn't legal tender in Charmington. Could this be some kind of test run? Or something else?

"But Rooster caught Ace and Cassidy and whacked them on the head!" Tom added.

"Hmm. Yes, that's where I get confused. We can gather from Cassidy and Olly's accounts that Ace discovered Rooster was down here. Cassidy is sent for, and then we assume she and Ace go in to capture Rooster. But somehow, the *two* of them are overwhelmed by *one* person, despite having the advantage of surprise."

"Rooster had an *accomplice!*" Tomcat stressed. "Who snuck up behind!"

Ella's gaze darted involuntarily to the green stain at the foot of the stairs. "An accomplice... Quite so." She took out the notebook Doctor Hyde had given her and wrote underneath the notes she had made when at Olly's.

Rooster is on the loose. Alone or with an accomplice? Green and black stains?

"Is an Avalon dollar a lot of money?" Ella tapped the pencil to her lips. "Obviously, the note I have for safekeeping is valuable. But how does one dollar compare to a Charmington gold chip or a Nottingham silver pound? Ten gold chips to the dollar?"

"Goodness, no," Tomcat chuckled. "When was the last time you handled foreign cash? A single gold Charmington piece is a week's wages. An Avalon dollar will only buy a pie."

"Are you sure? I know that the banknote I took for safekeeping is highly valuable."

"Well, assuming it is a complete forgery and still seen as worth a dollar, then sure, it's valuable when, technically, it should be worthless."

Ella blinked. "All paper money should be worthless. I agree with Dirk there. He's quite right. It could be burned, blown away in the wind, or ruined if it was in a pocket on wash day! What a silly idea."

Should be wasn't the same as *was*, though. And that meant those one-hundred-dollar banknotes stuffed in Cassidy's jacket were worth a lot to the right person. Each note was equivalent to a week's wages. Had Cassidy picked them up as evidence? Or for some other reason...? The word *bribe* floated into her thoughts again.

One thing was sure, she was going to have to find and question other people who had heard that argument between Ace and Cassidy.

"We'll have to keep watch over this place!" Tomcat said, standing up on his hind legs as the idea occurred. "I can sit on the haberdashery porch and watch for any comings and goings! Rooster has to plan on coming back, right? It's the only reason I can think of for moving the bodies when no one would have found them here." He rubbed a paw over a furry arm. "And I have the best disguise ever!"

Tom did have an interesting point. Why move the bodies? Obviously, the printing press couldn't be moved due to its weight. And, as Tom said, whoever had been using it would come back, and it would become extremely unpleasant in here quickly if they didn't remove the bodies... But why move them all the way to the post office?

"Oh! Hillary's key!" Ella gasped as the memory of the early council meeting popped into her mind.

"Sorry, what?" Tom asked.

"Hillary said she dropped her key after leaving work last night because the streetlamps were out, and she tripped over a couple of times."

"Ahh! And Rooster must have seen her do it! That's why he moved the bodies there!"

"Yes, it does add up. Finding the key would have been excellent timing when he had bodies to dispose of that he didn't want found. The labyrinth of post office basements *should* have been a perfect hiding place, until we accidentally stumbled along, of course..." Ella said thoughtfully to herself. "Our finding the bodies certainly must have ruined someone's plan... I can't imagine they were put there to be found. Maybe to follow up on this theory, you could hunt for the key along the street, in between keeping an eye on this place, because if you do find the key, we can rule out that possibility. And, while you do that, I will report that Rooster is on the loose to Axel. What do you say?"

Naturally, she could also question Axel about *his* whereabouts last night at the same time! She hadn't forgotten that he had walked Hillary home.

Tomcat nodded. "Great plan! Now you're thinking like a guardsman!"

"How delightful," Ella replied flatly, and gestured for Tomcat to climb the ladder ahead of her. As his little paws clambered up the steps, Ella took the opportunity to write in her notebook: *Suspects: Rooster. Axel.*

After a moment, she added: *Cassidy?*

Then she closed the leather cover and climbed back up the steps into daylight.

CHAPTER 12

AXEL INTERVIEW

Her walking stick tucked under one arm, Ella strode purposefully through the narrow alley between the abandoned cluckoo shop and the twins' haberdashery. Goodness, this newfound physical capacity improved her mood. Even with all the awful events this morning, today at least she could stride along without having the pain in her knees remind her of her frailties.

However, on reaching Northgate Square, Ella leaned heavily on her stick once more, as if each step were laboured. If Axel was involved in faking money, or some other terrible predicament in which Cassidy and Ace had found themselves entangled, she would have to tread very carefully—both literally and figuratively. Therefore, ensuring that Axel carried on his assumption that she was nothing but a harmless old biddy was to her advantage...

On approaching the former café, now the police station, located directly within the town gates, Ella spied Harold in a discussion with Axel. The pair were standing beside a new noticeboard covered in many 'Wanted persons' and 'Magic is forbidden' types of posters.

Harold turned and caught her eye. He bid good day to the sheriff and stomped past Ella, saying, "You're too late, as always. I have already reported the fight between the night's watch *and* them breaking into the post office."

Ella just managed a tight smile of acknowledgement. Harold might well feel smug in beating her to report the incident, but she doubted the postmaster had questioned Axel over *his* alibi...

With a broad smirk, Axel bent down and picked up another rolled poster, which he proceeded to tack onto the board with a little brass hammer.

Ella stopped in her tracks when glancing at the poster, which read: *Reward. 50 golds for the capture of a talking cat. Dead or alive.*

"Fifty!" Ella blurted, astonished at both the contents of the poster and the amount of the reward. That was a year's wages, according to young Tom.

"Well, well, Granny Charming," Axel gloated, running his palm over the paper to help flatten it out. "If I'd known getting you to hand over your talking cat was going to be this easy, I wouldn't have commissioned so many posters." He gestured to a little cart nearby, filled to the brim with rolled-up tubes of paper.

"I don't know what you're on about," Ella huffed, tight-lipped. "I don't *own* a talking cat." Certainly, that was true. Technically, she didn't own Tom. Her cat Tilly, inside whom young Tom had found his conscious mind trapped, was entirely of the non-magical kind right up until the shooting star incident two months ago.

"Sure, you don't," Axel intoned, his voice dismissive. "Not that I expected you to be enticed by the reward anyways." His horrid grin broadened. "But it will tempt everyone else…"

Ella's fingers tightened across the silver head of her walking cane as she regarded the reward poster again. "Dead or alive, eh? I rather think you'll shortly find yourself up to your ears in dead cats, swiftly followed by a deluge of cat lovers complaining that their kitty has gone missing." She returned a smug grin of her own. "Surely a talking cat, if such a thing existed, once deceased, is entirely indistinguishable from a run-of-the-mill cat? Or didn't that occur to you?"

Axel's eyes bulged as he regarded his poster again, and the reality hit home. The sheriff swore under his breath and muttered something about reprinting costs, but to Ella's relief, he ripped the poster down from the noticeboard and scrunched it into a tight ball. "How is young Tom April?"

"Beg pardon?" Ella blurted, stunned that Axel would be so direct after dancing around the issue with all his talking cat nonsense.

"Last night, when I walked Hillary home, she told me she saw Tom recovering at your cottage." He pitched the useless reward poster into the cart. "You really had me going, what with all that business that I had actually killed him."

Ella looked away as she gathered her wits. Magic preserve, had Axel truly not made the connection between his missing rookie henchman, Tom April, and the appearance of a talking cat?

But then again, what Hillary had actually seen last month was Wulf tucked up in Ella's feather bed with the bedclothes drawn up over his head while he pretended to be young Tom. Clearly the ruse had worked...

"Ahem, Tom is recovering slowly, and doesn't talk much. He's too weak."

Axel shrugged. "That's something, I guess...and that means I'm *not* a murderer. At any rate, tell Tom that his wages are being docked for absenteeism. Toddle on now before I arrest you for loitering."

"As agreeable as departing from your presence will be," Ella replied, "I'm here to report the sighting of a notorious criminal heralding from Nottingham. A one-eared chap, goes by the name of—"

"Rooster," Axel interrupted, finishing her sentence. "And as the fat little postmaster just said, you're too late. I arrested Rooster a couple of days ago." Axel waved a hand in the direction of the barred windows of the former café's basement, which had been used to store barrels of wine and beer. "He's down in the cells as we speak."

"What? A couple of days ago?" Ella was stunned. Magic preserve. If that were true it entirely threw out the timeline of events that Ella and Tom had deduced. "Can I speak to him?"

"What?" Axel baulked, apparently as surprised as Ella had been. "No, you can't *talk* to him! One, he's a dangerous criminal, and two, this isn't tax-related..." Axel's beratement trailed off as they both heard the distinctive clink of empty bottles coming from the station's stable yard. The sheriff stormed off to investigate, and Ella found herself trailing after him.

What exactly would happen if Axel were to discover that the talking cat he had encountered *was* Tom April? Would he try to get his former employee back serving on the guards? Certainly, having a spy in cat form would open up a lot of possibilities for someone with as dubious a reputation as the new sheriff...

"What do you think you're doing?" Axel demanded, striding up to a slim figure wrapped in a scarlet cloak, who was currently loading a small handcart with empty bottles that had been discarded willy-nilly about the stable yard—no doubt detritus from the previous night's celebratory promotion party.

The figure swept back their hood, revealing an attractive, heart-shaped face surrounded by a swirl of dark curls. Robinne, Ella's nearest neighbour, who also lived deep within Wyld Enchantment woods. "What does it look like I'm doing?" She casually tipped out a half-finished beer onto the icy cobbles.

"It looks like you're stealing my empty bottles," Axel reported, grabbing several bottles from her cart and chucking them onto snow drifts or on the cobbles, where they broke.

"Hey! I need those!" Robinne said, standing between him and the cart to shield the remaining bottles with her body. "They're not *yours*. They belonged to Arthur, and he let me buy empties off him."

"A likely story," Axel huffed, his arms crossed over his leather jerkin. "Don't think that I don't know that you're the thieving outlaw everyone calls the Red Unicorn. I could arrest you for that alone!"

"Didn't you *hang* the Red Unicorn?" Ella interjected. "I certainly recall the queen paying you a large bounty for the Unicorn's capture many years ago."

Axel looked abashed. "Well, I, sure, but that was the *old* Red Unicorn. There's a *new* one. Someone has been stealing shipments from the goods barges—Arthur had ordered and paid for a case of Mossfern whiskey, but it hasn't turned up. And that happens to be *my* favourite whiskey, and I want it back."

"Perhaps it's been delayed," Ella piped up, hoping to smooth things over. "And I'm sure the pair of you can come to a fair price for the bottles. What did Arthur charge you, my dear?"

"Two coppers a bottle," Robinne said, picking up another bottle and examining it for cracks.

"Ha!" Axel mocked, snatching the brown glass bottle from her hands. "The price is now one silver coin per bottle, and then we have a deal."

"One silver! But that's more than I sell my brew for!" Robinne snapped, and gesturing to the bottles collected in her cart, she added, "*You* didn't pay for any of these. They were all from Arthur's stock, anyway!"

Axel chose that moment to grab Robinne's elbow, stating, "You're under arrest on suspicion of being the Red—*urgh!*"

Robinne kneed the new sheriff in his vitals and made a break for it. She gave Ella a wink as she darted past, throwing a cheeky retort at the doubled-over sheriff, "Congrats on the promotion!"

Still clutching himself, Axel limped after the fleeing young woman, the words "*assault*" and "*under arrest*" puffing in clouds of steam against the frosty winter air.

"Magic preserve," Ella muttered, finding herself alone in the now-empty stable yard at the back of the café-come-police station. Not being one to ignore a gift horse—or timely fugitive chase in this case—she went to find the door that led down into the wine cellars.

What were the odds that Axel had been lying and that Rooster was most certainly *not* locked up below? "Quite high, I wager," Ella muttered to herself while knocking off the snow from her boots against the boot scraper at the back door. One thing was for sure, the day was getting more interesting with every hour.

CHAPTER 13

COCK–A–DOODLE–DOO

NEW POLICE STATION, NORTHGATE SQUARE, CHARMINGTON.

On any other day, Ella's plan to question Rooster might well have been stymied by the police staff blocking her entry to the former wine cellar, now prison cells. But this day, following a night of what surely must have been an attempt to drink the former café dry, the station was littered with sleeping bodies. The scene was quite eerie and reminded her of that time Merlin had overdone some potion or other and the whole castle had been put to sleep for several days.

Cautiously, she navigated through the people. There were castle guards, town guards, musicians, and various other townsfolk strewn about the place. Mistress Fairweather, a plump lady with a beetroot-red face, who ran the orphanage on Baker Street, was, unfortunately, sleeping sitting propped up against the wine-cellar door. Ella clasped Fairweather's elbow and was able to gently slide her out of the way with nothing more than a crack of eyes and a blurry mumble of, "I pay my taxes," when Ella's chain of office dangled in front of her bloodshot eyes.

A well-used but sturdy wooden ramp was beyond the door, and after a few hesitant moments, with the light on her walking stick engaged, she ventured down to the gloomy but warm and dry basement. Several of the large wine cellar alcoves with arched roofs had been partitioned off with new steel bars and doors. Only one of these newly fashioned prison cells was occupied. At the back of the windowless cell, a figure lay on a cot with his or her back to the opening. When the walking stick light played across the cell, casting long shadows over the stonework, the prisoner sat up, a hand raised to shield their eyes. But in that movement, Ella saw the pinkish scar tissue where an ear had been burned off—during a fire they had accidentally started when they broke into Gretel's tavern, or so Cassidy had informed Ella last month.

"Rooster," Ella said to herself, more a statement of confirmation than a question. So that part of Axel's story was true. How very disappointing.

"Who wants to know?" Rooster voiced, peering at her with a mix of cunning and suspicion.

He was a wretched-looking individual. Thin to the point of scrawny. His blond hair was more a dirty brown, and grown, or cut, to emphasise his name, judging from the central crest that rose to a point above his ruined ear. His clothes were dingy, ill-fitting, and made up of several layers, which was not surprising given the temperatures outside. Surprisingly, he did still have his boots, which appeared to be the most expensive thing he owned. Good quality and polished to a shiny black. He sat up and thumped his boots to the flagstone floor with a jingle.

Ah. So he had spurs on his boots, too. Another reference to his name and a nice touch, Ella conceded. Now, how to deal with him? In all honesty, Ella had thought Axel had been lying about the thief's incarceration and hadn't dreamed up any questions. She extracted her notebook from her pocket to stall for time.

This seemed to have a relaxing effect on Rooster. He slouched back against the stone cellar wall with a dismissive huff. "Reporter, huh? Ain't seen you around before. You new?"

Ella flipped through to a clean page in Doctor Hyde's notebook. "How long have you been in here?"

Rooster shook his pointy crest of hair and shrugged. "I don't know, do I? What's it to you, anyway?"

Ella ignored the question and pressed on. "How did you end up here?"

Rooster rolled his eyes in disgust. "How long have I been here? Why am I here? Is this your first day? 'Cuse me, Missus, but I fink you oughta go back to knitting and stuff. Reporting ain't your game."

Ella glowered and turned away. Knitting! Always with the knitting! She turned back to the cell and gasped. Rooster was standing right beside her at the bars. She hadn't heard him move, even with the spurs!

"Haha!" he laughed, seeing her flinch. "Yeah, I'm a speedy one!" Running a hand through his spiked hair, he added, "Consider that a free lesson. Don't turn your back on no one, or you wind up dead. Lesson two, you wants to interview a notorious high-level criminal mastermind like meself, then bring a pie or sumfing! A clean shirt! I ain't spilling my guts for free."

Ella swallowed and schooled her face as best she could. "My apologies, you are quite right. I will be back in a moment..."

Aware she probably didn't have a lot of time, Ella ventured back upstairs and fossicked around in the kitchen. Fortunately, the larder was still very well stocked, even despite the shenanigans of the night before, and she was able to rustle up a pound of cheese, a pot of blackcurrant jam, and a tub of what she suspected was candied walnuts.

She laid them in front of Rooster's cell door, wise enough not to risk putting her hands through the bars to deliver them. Rooster gathered up the offerings and went to slouch on his cot once more at the back of the cell.

"Tell me about last night," Ella began.

"I don't remember last night," Rooster replied, a cheeky boyish grin on his narrow features.

"Who else can vouch for your whereabouts?" Ella tried again.

Rooster shrugged and picked at his fingernails. "Hard to say. I'm not good with names."

Ella sighed deeply. So, this was how it was going to be, was it? Playing games. Well, two could do that. She placed pencil to paper and wrote while saying aloud, "While being questioned about his activities, Rooster said, and I quote, 'After killing the two guards, I stuffed my pockets with as much paper money as I could before my associates noticed I had taken their share as well...'"

"Hey!" Rooster said. He sat bolt upright and stormed towards the cell door, his spurs jingling as if with indignation. "You can't write that. That ain't what happened. There was only one guard, and I ain't killed him!"

"Describe the guard to me, so I know you're telling the truth," Ella said, her voice laced with sympathy.

Rooster sliced a hand through the air at knee height. "Little guy, one of them magic types. You know, a maker."

That certainly sounded like Ace, but to be sure she added, "Did he have glasses or maybe a uniform?"

"Yeah, yeah, little pink glasses and all. I ain't sure about a uniform." Rooster swiped his hand up through his hair again, a nervous gesture that fanned the hair into a crest. Perhaps that was how he first got his name.

Ella made a show of crossing out her first lines and then said, "And why did you kill him?"

"I told you, I ain't killed no one!" He gripped the bars and glared. "I'm *trying* to go straight. It's me luck, see. Me *bad* luck, I can't shake it. I can't go back to prison, I can't!"

Ella waved the pencil, pointing out the former wine cellar in which they stood. "But...you're in prison...?"

Rooster tilted his head back, and he laughed gruffly. "This ain't prison. This is some soft lock-up. I'd do a lag here and no complaint. Nottingham is a *real* prison. I step in there, and her gang will kill me."

"Whose gang?"

Rooster turned away and stalked back to his cot. "Talking is over. No one crosses the Mrs. and lives."

Ella looked up as pounding footsteps crossed the floorboards above, accompanied by the distinctive sound of Axel's voice, cursing the escape of young Robinne. "That's my cue to leave... Enjoy the jam."

Perhaps it was because of being reminded of the food stuffs, or just because, but Rooster offered one last piece of advice as she turned to go, saying, "You want to find out what happened to the little guy? Follow the money."

CHAPTER 14

THE QUEEN'S SHOCKING ROYAL DECREE

Unicorn Water Fountain, Northgate Square, Charmington.

A few minutes later, her ear pressed to the old wine cellar door until she was certain that Axel had ventured upstairs or gone elsewhere, Ella tip-toed out of the basement. People were stirring, no doubt awoken by Axel's stomping around and noisy cursing, and she was able to exit the police station among two or three rather hungover party-goers, who paid her no mind.

Out in Northgate Square, there were more people than Ella was expecting. In fact, quite a crowd was gathering in front of the steps of the town hall.

Goodness, perhaps there was going to be an announcement that the town hall and post office were being shut for the day due to what had occurred there this morning? But would that attract such a crowd?

Fortunately, the milling people gave Ella an excuse to pause beside the iced-over unicorn fountain in the middle of the square, and she jotted down *Follow the money* in her notebook. Tapping her pencil against the pages, she took a moment to think about what she had learned that morning which was 'money' related.

First, there had been some argument between Cassidy and Ace about bribes. That could certainly be tied to money. If she could find other people who had heard that argument, it might be worthwhile to double-check Hillary and Harold's versions of the wording. After all, bribes could be anything depending on the situation, as she had witnessed, from a simple pot of jam to a promotion.

She sighed. The foreign banknotes remained a thorn. What exactly did their presence in Cassidy's pockets imply? Depending on how one looked at it, they could be bribes, but just as likely, if not more, given Cassidy's job and reputation, the banknotes could have been collected as evidence. But evidence of what?

Were they genuine Avalon banknotes, or had they been printed on the press she and Tom uncovered? As Tom had observed, there were no printing plates, which meant they couldn't confirm the theory that the notes *were* fakes. Ella hummed as she thought and stamped her feet as the frosty air seeped into her bones.

Might there be some skilled individual in Charmington who could discern a real banknote from a forged one? Possibly someone working at the bank? Yes, she should take some of the hundred-dollar notes to the bank. Ella patted her pocket, but then remembered that Dirk had stuffed all the hundreds into his tricorn. She'd have to go back to the hospital and collect some.

"Good morn', your ladyship," said a warm familiar voice, and Ella lifted her head from her notes and her musing to see Martha Chelton, the butcher's wife, approach the fountain, set her clay pipes to lips, and then jet a puff of peppermint-scented clouds into the air.

"Good morning, Martha. Oh, and to you as well, Master Chelton," Ella added, acknowledging with some surprise that the well-dressed man beside Martha was her husband, Chelton, the butcher. Ella blinked. She rarely saw the butcher without his sleeves rolled up and his blue and white striped apron about his neck. Today, he wore a suit jacket. He even had a bowler hat and a purple necktie. He looked quite dapper, although rather uncomfortable.

He nodded *good morning* in return. And tugged on the necktie he wasn't used to wearing. Ella wondered what the occasion might be for the outfit. A wedding anniversary?

"We were expecting to see you up there, not down here with the common folks," Martha chuckled and pointed with her clay pipe up at the top of the town hall steps. Some castle guards were rolling out a red carpet, and a few others carrying trumpets were positioning themselves on either side of the main doors. A man with a very formal black jacket and tie, dressed as if he were about to attend the opera in one of the big cities, was using a baton to cajole a bunch of children into formation. Ella realised it must be a choir.

Cheapcuts, the Cheltons' son, whose real name was Chelton Junior, was among the choir, and he gave his parents a shy wave.

What was with all the pomp? Ella groaned. "Oh dear, is there going to be a royal decree?"

Martha chuckled as if Ella had been joking. "I always like to get in early, get a good spot, don't you?"

"Uh huh," Ella replied, looking about the gathering townsfolk and wondering how obvious it would be if she slunk off. Royal announcements were long and tedious and only designed to give Sibylla justification for the purchase of another elaborate gown, as far as Ella could determine.

Martha was casting Ella little glances, as if she wanted to ask something, but was being respectfully reserved. Ella took the opportunity to prompt her. "Are you all well? I didn't know Cheapcuts could sing."

Chelton pulled a sceptical face, as if that matter was still up for debate.

"Aye, no, singing isn't one of the boy's talents, to be fair," Martha replied stoically. "This was the best they could do on short notice. Typically, Mistress Fairweather has her orphans do the honours, only she weren't available."

Ella thought about having seen Mistress Fairweather at the police station, sleeping off a drunken night. "Indeed... Speaking of Cheapcut's *other* talents, those we discussed last month, I'm still waiting to hear back from Merlin about the possibility of a scholarship."

Perhaps that was what was on the couple's minds. Martha had confided that their son was displaying some magical abilities, and Ella had offered to find out if the school Merlin taught at in Avalon would take the boy.

"Very kind of you. We're honoured you'd ask, but we don't expect anything. Fancy school like that..." Martha chewed the end of her clay pipe.

Chelton nudged his wife and then nodded at Ella, as if trying to coax his wife or jog her memory. Chelton never spoke, but he and his wife seemed to communicate very well, nonetheless.

Martha's lips pressed tight, as if she was debating whether to bring up the topic they clearly wanted to ask.

Ella sighed. If it wasn't Cheapcut's education, then there was one topic she could well interpret to be on the couple's mind and took the moment to pre-empt the conversation. "I'm afraid it's true," she told the couple. "The rents are going to be tripled."

This announcement drew a rippled gasp from other people nearby, who had also gathered around the frozen water fountain.

"Easy for some," a disgruntled voice snaked out from the crowd. "We ain't all dripping with gold."

Chelton straightened from his slouched gloom in being forced to wear his Sunday best and stood up to his full height. Goodness, he really was an extremely large man. He had the height and breadth of a bear.

As if attempting to temper down any ill will that might direct at Ella herself, Martha said loudly, as if to no one in particular, "The rents have always been fair. Would be a dishonourable assumption to say that still ain't so. I have no doubt there are sound and justifiable reasons for their increase."

Hmm, Ella couldn't deny the truth of that. In a way, the citizens had brought it upon themselves. They were the ones who wanted magic banned all those years ago. When Mrs. Haversham spread her black magic plague that targeted humans, the townsfolk decided magic was the true culprit. They reasoned that if there was no magic, good or bad, then it couldn't be used against others.

But twenty years without magic in an economy built on magic meant the town was suffering. No sales of magical goods and trade meant no thriving local businesses or even foreign money from those who travelled to spend time at the spas or have their children educated here. Charmington was on the cusp of bankruptcy. What would happen if the townsfolk found out? Who might they turn against then?

She ran the chain of office through her fingers and had a terrible notion it might be her...

While she was brooding, Martha and Chelton idly wandered, as if they were just positioning to get a better view of the town steps, but somehow managed to end up standing protectively on either side of Ella. Martha gave her a nod and smile, a gesture of friendship that Ella found no small comfort in.

A castle guard dressed in a formal livery of a purple frock coat with shiny golden buttons opened the town hall's twin doors, and the crowd's attention was drawn from Ella to the top of the steps.

Ella took the time to think over what else she remembered that might be useful about the banknotes that were now secured in Dirk's tricorn. Certainly, the colour of the notes was very similar, if not the exact same green colour, as the ink smeared on the old *Charmington Chatter* newspapers with the press, as was the one-dollar note she had in her pocket. But that note also had a black splotch—and come to think of it, while there were plenty of green ink-type stains down in the basement, there had also been a small amount of black residue too.

Black on the cluckoo shop basement floor, black on the torn one-dollar note, and, as Ella had witnessed, black stains running down poor little Ace's chin. Could someone have attempted to drown him in a vat of black ink or dye? If so, where was such a vat? Was there a dye works in town?

She turned back to look at the police station and saw that Axel was standing in one of the upper windows, glaring down at her. Axel had been telling the truth that he did have Rooster, Ella's main suspect, locked up. And surely, if Axel himself were somehow involved in Ace's death and Cassidy's head wound, he would have simply said, *'I caught Rooster red-handed attacking members of the watch and promptly arrested him.'*

But Axel had claimed that Rooster had been imprisoned a few days ago. Which made Rooster look innocent, at least according to the timeline of last night that *both* Olly and Cassidy had said independently of each other.

A dark thought crossed Ella's mind. *Could* Cassidy be guilty? No, surely not. That couldn't be true. But perhaps Axel was trying to make Cassidy look guilty? But how? After all, they had stumbled upon the bodies in the basement—a locked room—by complete coincidence. Those bodies hadn't been put there to be found. They had been concealed.

Ella shook her head. What evidence did she really have against Axel other than a known dislike of Cassidy and a green stain on his boots?

It wasn't enough.

And what was more likely? That Rooster, a self-proclaimed notorious criminal mastermind, was innocent of killing Ace? Or that the new sheriff, who had no known grudge against Ace, had done it? Rooster had given a clear description of the little craftsman. That made him look guilty. Unless Rooster was taking the fall for Axel's crimes?

Ella shook her head. Just when everything had been adding up, it all fell apart again. Someone was lying, but who?

The crowd's alert attention was waning as nothing else had happened in the minutes the town hall doors had opened. Ella whispered to Martha, "Are there any dye works in town?"

Martha sucked on her clay pipe contemplatively. "There be a few people who will take in items of clothing and such to dye and mend, but nothing on a larger scale, if that's what you're asking." She leaned forward to speak with her husband, who was still standing protectively beside Ella and casting narrowed-eyed looks at any citizen who even looked like they were about to cause trouble. "My love, can you think of any?"

Chelton made a shrug and a complicated hand gesture. Martha tutted as if she should have known whatever he'd just communicated. "Aye, the nearest is Nottingham. We used to have one on Hot Cockle Lane, before the big winter. But, with the cold and all, the building has become a popular place to live due to the thermal vents. Free heating, you see."

"Families are living in an old dyehouse?" Ella rocked back on her heels. "All crammed in?"

She had been about to say *That doesn't sound very hygienic* when she sensed the darkening mood of the people around her. Many faces regarded her with open contempt. Times were tough, and everyone knew it. They were doing what they had to. Not everyone had a snug little cottage in the Wyld Enchantment Woods and no concern about where their next meal was coming from...

At that moment, the trumpeters standing on either side of the door raised their instruments to their lips and blasted out a stirring round of notes. The man dressed for the opera raised his baton, and a dozen children's reedy voices filled the air with a watery rendition of *Our Wyld hearts beat untamed and free.* A crowd favourite that always left the citizens with a glow of patriotism.

Ella gulped. If Sibylla was laying it on this thick, she must have a truly horrific announcement. Was she actually going to tell all these people that their country was in financial ruins?

Magic preserve, just when this day couldn't get any worse!

Ella held her breath as the queen's entourage preceded her. The ladies-in-waiting dressed in blue silks all fanned out across the steps, like a sea of beauty in which the queen herself was the brightest pearl dressed in purest white.

Ella had a rather jaded thought that all those ladies-in-waiting were more bodies that separated Sibylla from the masses should things turn ugly.

Sibylla strutted out in an elegant white gown trimmed with fur, and the citizens all bowed in one smooth motion, leaving Ella stunned and standing upright like the only corn stalk that had survived the harvest. On any other day, she would have stood her ground, but today she bowed low. Standing out did not seem like a very smart move when, clearly, something extremely nasty was about to go down.

"Beloved citizens of Charmington," Sibylla's clear voice rang out, pure and strong, and if it wasn't for the fact Ella knew Sibylla had never executed a decent *captivation* charm in her life, Ella would have thought her sister was using magical enhancement in her speech.

"In honour of the visit of the Camelot Academy Press delegation next month," Sibylla declared, "in which the world's most eminent magician, my beloved brother Merlin, will be gracing us with his presence to celebrate the commemorative edition printing of his masterpiece, *The Guide to Creatures of Wyld Kingdom*. A book of which I know all Charmington citizens are rightly proud. I, Sibylla Prudence Steadfast Winifred Charming, rightful queen of Wyld Kingdom, hereby decree that next month there shall be a complete magical amnesty. To ensure the comfort of our noble guests, all forms of magic are to be reinstated for one month. All magical goods and the sale of said goods shall incur no fines or repercussions…"

Whatever else Sibylla said to round up the speech, Ella didn't hear in the sudden rise of stunned murmuring voices.

Magic preserve, that was unexpected. Next month, magic was going to be allowed back in Wyld Kingdom!

CHAPTER 15

DESPERATION AND ILLUMINATION

As the crowds dispersed, Ella went to search for Tom to see if he had found the lost post office key. She trudged through the snowdrifts along the narrow avenue that ran from the town hall to the bank.

A small, unobtrusive door, one of many connected to the back of the post office, opened, and Hillary ventured out into the cold daylight, a cardboard box balanced against her hip. She pulled the door closed and proceeded down the cobblestones, a distinctive clink of bottles rattling with her every step.

Hmm, could this be the alcohol stash that has been in Harold's little drinking nook? The box the young woman lugged was plain cardboard, whereas the one in the storeroom was a wooden crate and had some branding stamped on it, but Ella couldn't recall what. Come to think of it, perhaps it would be a good idea to go and have another look around the storeroom?

Yes... Ella added that to her list of things to do. At the time, the room, other than clearly being a hidey-hole for someone to have a sly drink and chocolate indulgence, seemed to be nondescript, a random spot to hide the bodies, but appearances could be deceptive. She would go fetch Tom, and they could both have a look for clues. Two sets of eyes were better than one.

Hillary glanced back on hearing Ella's footfall behind and stopped walking so Ella could catch up to her. "Good Mother Ella, I was hoping to bump into you."

"Good day, Miss Harper. Are you heading home? I expect your father has given you the morning off after that terrible discovery in the basement."

Hillary merely pulled a face that said *How poorly you know my father*. "He didn't give me the day off when mother died, so..." She let the implication hang.

Goodness, Harold was worse than Ella ever could have imagined. No wonder he didn't give Hillary a promotion. Why would he encourage her to higher things when he had such a convenient dogsbody to boss around?

Hillary appeared to shrug off any regrets of her own and said blithely, "Congratulations on your new job. Are you having an office party?"

Ella blinked. "A party?" She ran the chunky gold chain through her gloved fingers. It hadn't occurred to her that congratulations were in order—commiserations, certainly. Magic preserve, who would welcome being the tax collector or covet such a job? Surely, no one in their right mind.

"Oh, yes," Hillary carried on. "You invite close friends and new colleagues up to your office. It's a bit like a housewarming party. Drinks, nibbles, all very civilised. Not like what the sheriff did. I wasn't trying to imply *you* would have *that* kind of rowdy party! Is Tom well enough to come? He has been in my thoughts."

"Ah, well, a party, I'll consider it. It would have to be a bit last minute. But, no, I'm afraid Tom is still under the weather and not fit for company."

"That's a shame. You will let me know the first sign he might like a *proper* visitor?" She readjusted the bulky crate on her hip. "That reminds me, there's mail for both you and Tom at the post office. There's a rather large parcel for you. It only came in on the Avalon barge a few days ago."

"Mail for me from Avalon?" Ella frowned. She was expecting a letter from her brother Merlin, but, surely, he wouldn't be sending a parcel? Whatever could it be?

Hillary set her box down. "Forgive me for being bold, but do you think you might be taking on any clerks?"

"Clerks?"

"Yes, for the tax office. I'm very good with numbers. And, well, if *you* requested me personally, I don't see how my father could refuse." She smiled brightly, a brittle edge of desperation hidden just behind her cheerful words. "Just say you'll think about it? I'd be ever so grateful." She nodded in the direction she was going. "This is where we part ways. Good day."

Ella watched the lass carry on lugging the heavy crate and felt a rising surge of sympathy for the poor child. Hillary was a bit odd, certainly. Ella sometimes felt like Hillary was reading her conversation from a playbook, as if she'd already decided how people should answer. But who wouldn't be a tad peculiar with such a father?

And if Hillary were good with numbers, then she might be a real asset to have on board the tax team. But then again, how would Harold react if Ella took away his assistant? He might make things very awkward and perhaps more miserable for Hillary than they already were.

Ella sighed. Many people would assume Hillary had a life of privilege, a father in a well-respected office and a grand house on East Avenue, but assumptions were fraught with error....

Tutting to herself, Ella turned the corner from the post office onto the back avenue. She came up behind Mistress Fairweather, who was berating Mr. Beau, the shoeshine man and lamplighter.

"I pay my taxes!" Mistress Fairweather was scolding Mr. Beau, who stood cap in hand, as she drew her shawl tight across her broad bosom. The movement made something clink. "I had to sleep over at the police station because the lamps were out after the party—it's a disgrace!"

"Yes, ma'am, sorry, ma'am," Mr. Beau responded, downcast, his boot polish blackened fingers peeking out from the short grey home-knitted fingerless gloves he wore. "I'm checking all the lamps along this row for tampering. Won't happen again."

"See that it doesn't," she sniffed haughtily, but then, on realising Ella was behind her, she started as if frightened. Without acknowledging Ella's presence, she scuttled away. The clink of glass on glass revealed two full bottles of ale tucked under her arms, only partly hidden by the shawl. Goodness, it seemed everyone today was trying to smuggle drinks. Whatever had become of the townsfolk!

"Phew!" Mr. Beau grinned and swept his cap back in place, wafting the air with a turpentine odour of Iron Drake boot polish that typically clung about him. He grinned. "Good morn', marm. You have done me a good turn, scaring off Mrs. F. like that—I tell you, once she gets a bee in her bonnet, I'm in for ten minutes or more of her tongue lashing."

"Hmm, is that so?" Ella muttered, wondering exactly what about her had frightened Mistress Fairweather, because she had to agree. It certainly did appear that the matron was shaken. Ella ran the golden official chain of office through her fingers. Quite likely, this insignia was the culprit. Tax collectors were never welcome.

Mr. Beau knelt at the base of a tall streetlamp and, with a little pocketknife, flipped open a brass hatch at the base. Ella leaned over to peer at what he was examining.

Mr. Beau clasped a small valve and turned it counterclockwise. There was a distinct hiss and a momentary waft of gas. "Aye, someone has shut off the valve. This can't happen by itself." He drew out a polishing rag from his coat pocket and buffed the inside of the hatch plate to a bright brass gleam. Clearly, this was a man who took pride in his work. Shining a part of the apparatus no one would ever see.

"And you think it's tampering? Who might do such a thing? The lamps benefit everyone, surely?" Ella voiced her concerns.

"Tampering is a strong word," he said with a chuckle. "I just said that to brighten the Mrs.' day with some gossip to repeat to her lady friends." He waved in the general direction that Mistress Fairweather had waddled off. "Nah, this is most like some drunken mischief. Proper tampering with intent would be damaging the gas line, see." He stood up and wiped his gloved hands across his thick winter coat. "No harm, no foul."

Ella thinned her lips. Did that mean he wasn't aware of the attack on the watch? But then again, she had drawn the conclusion that the handy cover of darkness had been linked to the attack on Ace...somehow. Maybe it was merely a coincidence?

"Is there a way to tell what time it was shut off?" she enquired.

Mr. Beau regarded her with a quizzically raised eyebrow. "There ain't no way to tell, ain't magic after all, but I know this row was lit up at half eleven when I left the party. Heard the town hall clock chime, and all, I swear on my job. Baker Bron was walking with me, and Dirk Turpin, come to think of it. You can ask them if it pleases you."

"Does everyone know how to turn them off?" Ella questioned, squinting up at the tall man.

"Ain't common knowledge as such," Mr. Beau admitted. "Looks easy, but there's a bit of a knack to it. You got to pull the lever *out* while you turn it. Only those trained know that. Members of the watch and such, in case there's a house fire nearby. Safer to shut off the line, you see. And, typically, the night watch shift will turn them down to a quarter light after one in the morning to save the gas."

Ella nodded. She glanced down the avenue and saw Olly for a brief moment, their head peering out between the railing of the haberdashery verandah. On being spotted, they ducked back as if they didn't want to be caught spying. That was odd, but Ella shrugged it off. Movement further along caught her eye, and she watched Tom, white fur on white snow, digging with little paws in a snowdrift at a pillar at the base of the bank.

Mr. Beau coughed. "Did you hear about that watch lassie, young Cassidy?"

"I did indeed." Ella returned her attention to the shoe shiner. "I haven't had any dealings with the doctor. Have you? Is he any good?"

Mr. Beau's lips pushed out in a shrug. "Aye, I only hear good things about Doctor Hyde. Heard he wrote a book and all. Got to be good if he's a literary type, is my thinking…"

Ella scrunched her nose. In her experience, writers were squirrelly types. Either a bit needy or a bit boastful. Her brother Merlin, when he wrote his now infamous *The Guide to Creatures of Wyld Kingdom,* had forever been trying her patience with tedious questions about the interactions between woodland dwelling animals and plants they consumed.

"I am glad to hear that Cassidy is in capable hands." Ella nodded.

Again, Mr. Beau's eyebrow quirked, as if he and Ella had been having two very different conversations. "Beg pardon, marm, but perhaps you haven't heard. Katie came past before and told me herself. She's working at the police station now and overheard Harold and his lawyer. Harold is pressing charges. Claims Cassidy broke into the post office. She's going to be transported to Nottingham prison first thing tomorrow morning."

CHAPTER 16

ONE CAT'S TREASURE
IS ELLA'S JUNK...

ALLEY BEHIND NORTHGATE SQUARE SHOPS, CHARMINGTON.

"Transported!" Ella repeated, utterly horrified, clutching her cloak tight to her throat. Her conversation with Rooster echoed in her mind. Nottingham prison. A *real* prison. A dangerous place to begin with, but more so for Cassidy. No doubt she had sent many local felons to be incarcerated there. "But why isn't Cassidy simply detained here until she can stand trial? We have a brand-new lock-up."

Mr. Beau ducked his head. "I'm just a shoeshine man. Best ask the sheriff." He touched his cap and excused himself.

"The sheriff!" Ella muttered under her breath. "The sheriff!" Of course! Her temper boiled, and she had to physically restrain herself from stamping her foot. Now things were starting to make sense. Axel *needed* Rooster to look innocent of any involvement in the attack on Ace if he wanted to pin all the blame on Cassidy to get her out of the way.

Last month, Cassidy had said she thought Axel was turning a blind eye to local smugglers. Maybe the sheriff was in league with the smugglers and lining his own pockets? Maybe Axel had planted that paper money on Cassidy? Axel could have known that basement room was Harold's private drinking nook!

Ugh! That awful, awful man. And she thought Harold was a toad! He paled in comparison to Axel. Why on earth had Sibylla put such a man in a trusted position of authority? And to think Sibylla had accused Ella of being blinded by Richard's lies when here she was being equally blind. Of all the hypocrisy!

There was only one thing to be done. Ella drew a deep, fortifying breath, sucking the frosty winter air into her lungs. The day wasn't over. She had just under twenty-four hours to prove Cassidy's innocence and expose Axel's devious plan.

Turning about, she stomped down the avenue toward Tom, who was digging quite a deep hole in the snowdrift at the base of the bank, his little tail waving like a flag. She glanced at the haberdashery veranda as she passed. Olly was there, but they ducked out of sight again. They were right: yellow velvet was not stealthy at all. But why try to hide from her? She shook it off. No doubt Tom had put some notion in the child's mind about how a spy should behave.

The fresh powdery snow crunched and impacted under her boots, and the ornate and yet solid Roman-style pillars of the grand old bank loomed above her, blocking all sunlight across the avenue. Ella was a little surprised by the architectural attention to detail, as this side of the building was the employee entrance to the bank. But then again, Charmington Castle presented a grand facade from every angle. Why shouldn't the bank also? After all, they were both institutions trying to maintain an aura of wealth and grandeur. Ella gritted her teeth at the irony. To think that the crown was in financial ruins! No one would ever suspect it. She huffed a breath. More hypocrisy.

"Ella!" said Tomcat, peeping out of his snowdrift. He jumped nimbly from the hole and pranced over to an upturned crate littered with an odd collection of junk. "Look at all the neat stuff I found! A penny whistle. Dice. Or is one a die? I can never remember. Three copper coins. Half a pencil. A rock with a hole in it—they're lucky, and—"

"But no keys?" Ella interrupted and pointed back to the hole he had dug in the snow pile at the foot of the bank.

"Ah, no, no keys." Tomcat ducked his head and his ears flattened as he glanced a little guiltily at the snowdrift. "I heard a mouse. Sorry, it was instinct. I couldn't resist."

"Never mind that. We've got to head back to the hospital." Ella turned about and forged ahead with Tomcat trailing and casting regretful looks at having to leave the lucky rock and other treasures behind.

"Did you report the sighting of Rooster?" Tomcat asked.

"I certainly did," Ella answered, refraining from informing him that Rooster was already under lock and key and theoretically hadn't been out roaming the streets last night.

Ella felt a prick in her conscience. A lie of omission was still a lie. But if Tom likewise came to the same conclusion that Axel was now their prime suspect, then he would go face off with the sheriff. That would most certainly end with Tom being captured and even less help to Cassidy's plight. She was doing it for his own good.

CHAPTER 17

THE DOCTOR KNOWS BEST

CHARITY HOSPITAL, HOT COCKLE LANE, CHARMINGTON.

A half-hour later, on entering the Hot Cockle Lane Charity Hospital, Ella was again momentarily disoriented by the sudden change in lighting from the bright glare of the winter day to the gloomy warehouse interior with patchwork shards of light. Tomcat, with his superior animal eyesight, darted ahead, his white bushy tail making a beeline for Cassidy's cot, where there appeared to be an argument between Dirk Turpin and two other men. One was in a guard's uniform. Oh dear.

Ella made her way through the rows of cots, passing Nigella Pickford, the actress, with the broken leg in plaster, and her hired nurse, Marge the midwife. Marge was now awake and sitting up and sipping a hot beverage, her gaze glued upon the argument across the way.

"Oh! Did you happen to get the *Nottingham Times*?" Nigella asked.

Ella extracted the decades-old copy of the *Charmington Chatter* from her skirt pocket and handed it over. "I'm afraid I had no time, but perhaps this might prove an entertaining distraction?"

Nigella's eyes lit up on reading the provoking headline. "*The Curse of the Scottish Play! What's that? How intriguing!*" She accepted the old paper with very good grace. Seemingly old news was good news when one was incapacitated and reading material was in short supply.

"Good morning, Lady Ella," Marge cooed, her cheeks dimpled in a smile of welcome. Though her usually neat curls were mussed up, she still exuded an air of a pretty little china doll. "How noble of your ladyship to spend your precious time tending to these *poor* wretches." If the midwife noticed the sudden muttered grumbling from the actress beside her who Marge herself was supposed to be attending, she paid no attention. Marge pointed to the growing argument surrounding Cassidy's hospital bed. "Did you hear about that? Guilty, guilty, guilty," Marge trilled, her angelic dimpled cheeks a façade to the malice she elated over. "I heard it myself. I was just telling Nigella."

"Beg pardon?" Ella asked, glancing up as Doctor Hyde marched out of his office and stood between Dirk and the other men to keep them apart.

Marge's eyes lit up, as if delighted to be able to inform Ella of the latest gossip circling the township. "Ace and Cassidy had a terrible row last night! Ace accused her of taking bribes! Witnessed it myself, didn't I, Nigella?"

"Uh huh," murmured Nigella, extracting a set of reading glasses from the bosom of her nightgown and paying more attention to the old newspaper than the unfolding drama before them.

Marge tutted. "And now Ace is dead!" She crossed her little plump arms as if the point had been made. "I can't see why they don't take her to prison right now. This is a respectable hospital. We shouldn't have to bunk with murderers!"

"Tosh, 'tis but Act One," the actress countered knowingly, as if they'd had this argument before. She lowered her reading glasses and peered contemplatively at Ella and Marge. "A good play holds its dramatic twists for the end! I shall not pick a villain yet."

Marge rolled her eyes. "This is real life! It all adds up. It doesn't take a genius to see what happened!" She shook her head as if they would just have to mark her words. "Go ask Robinne if you don't believe me. She heard the fight between Ace and Cassidy, too. Ask a well-known thief if you put more stock in her word than mine, a well-respected member of the community." Marge puffed herself up like an indignant sparrow.

Ella left Marge to her voyeurism and Nigella to her newspaper and crossed the hospital floor to Cassidy's bedside, where Doctor Hyde was just in the progress of steering the guard and the other man, who, judging from the style of his buttoned-up jerkin, ill-fitting wig, and clutch of papers, was probably a lawyer, over to a quieter darkened corner of the hospital, where Gretel was sitting on deathbed watch.

Gretel's eyes narrowed at the sight of the bewigged lawyer, and her lips pulled back to emit a low hiss. Given that all of Gretel's pearly white teeth were canines, this had an immediate subduing effect on the quarrelling.

"Take this outside!" Doctor Hyde snapped, seizing the moment and drawing himself up to his full height. With the guard and lawyer momentarily dazed by Gretel's ominous hiss, he yanked both the lawyer and the guard toward the entrance. "The patient remains in my care and will not be released until tomorrow—that is my final word!"

After shoving the pair back out onto the street, which drew a round of applause from some of the patients, the doctor smoothed his duster and turned sharply on his heel. Catching Ella's eye, he pointed at her. "You! I want a word with you!"

"Me?" Ella gulped, taken aback like a guilty school child summoned to the headmaster's office, but, without further protest, she followed the bald doctor into his office. "I'm afraid I haven't had time to do anything about the funds for the roof. It has been quite a busy morning."

"Quite," said the doctor, his clipped tone conveying that she had *no idea* what a truly busy morning entailed. He ventured to a wide shelf on which a tea urn was sputtering and bubbling, and pointed to a chair for Ella to take in front of his desk, laden with folders of notes and several medical books. "Sit."

Ella slunk into the chair. On the desk, she spied an extremely fine and ornate copy of her brother Merlin's book, *The Guide to Creatures of Wyld Kingdom.*

Still with the air of being summoned into the staff room of her favourite teacher, Mrs. Haversham, Ella cast her gaze around the office to form a better understanding of the new doctor.

The former horses' tack room had many peculiar diagrams of body parts and skeletons. A rather grand formal certificate from the Avalon University put the jammy royal decree Ella had penned for Olly to shame.

"How do you have your coffee?" the doctor asked over his shoulder, ladling a fragrant and rather thick, black-looking potion into a mug.

"Er...? Coffee?" Ella found herself once more on the back foot. "What's that?"

The doctor blinked as if she'd said something truly ignorant. "Only the elixir of life." A corner of his lip curled, and Ella wondered if the doctor was making an attempt at humour. He shrugged, ladled more of the dark black liquid into another cup and set it before her, thumping it down on the grand edition of Merlin's book. "Black then, which is best, as the milk is off."

Ella lifted the cup from what she suspected was a first edition of *The Guide* as the Doctor threw himself onto his swivelling desk chair.

"Do you have a coaster, perhaps? I wouldn't want to spill anything onto your book."

"The book *is* the coaster," Doctor Hyde retorted. This time, the lip curl was definitely in honest disgust and not jest. Calling Merlin's encyclopaedia "the book" was tantamount to an insult in these parts, where it was particularly revered. Every family of above modest means had their own edition.

Oh my, thought Ella. Someone else who wasn't a fan of her brother's undeserved fame. *How refreshing.* Ella had a sip and thumped the cup squarely back on the first edition of *The Guide*. She liked Doctor Hyde all the more. "Oh, this is the roasted bean juice drink," she added, recognising the beverage once she had tasted it. "I had that in Constantinople! My sister Arabella introduced this bean juice stuff to me. It's very hard to come by here."

"Nearly impossible," the doctor conceded dolefully, as if she might not be such a country bumpkin as he had first assumed. Host duties apparently over, he asked, "Am I correct in the observation that you, Mistress...?"

"Charming," Ella supplied.

"Mistress Charming, are investigating the death of the night watchman, Mr. Ace?"

Ella sat back, surprised by his directness. "Oh well, I mean, not officially. But yes."

"Why?"

The blunt question once more caught Ella off guard.

"For the glory?" Doctor Hyde answered for her in the silence. "Or perhaps he was your friend?"

Ella thought about the reasons. There were many, but one stood above them all. "For the truth," she answered.

The doctor nodded, as if she had passed some kind of test. He opened a drawer on his desk and extracted a thin pocket-sized book with a red cover. The words *Rare Poisons and Their Antidotes by Dr. Edison Hyde* were emblazoned in gold foil.

"My goodness! *Rare Poisons and Their Antidotes.* That sounds very useful." Ella was impressed. "You must have sold thousands of copies."

The doctor's square, bony shoulders drooped. "I sold two dozen," he said with painful honesty.

"But," Ella protested, "but *how*?" She gestured to Merlin's *Guide*. "Merlin sold thousands, and his book is mostly a collection of common knowledge..." She trailed off as she caught the haunted look of a man resigned to the unfairness of the world. "Ah, I see. Merlin is a bit of a showman. His theatrics do appeal to the everyman."

"Quite," the doctor returned with his clipped tone. "We published in the same week and shared the same publisher, Camelot Academy Press... My subject matter was niche, limited market... I see that now." He shook himself, as if he had revealed far more than he intended, and abruptly changed topics. "You were there this morning, where the deceased and the injured party were found. What did you observe? Observation only, no conjecture."

Ella sat back in the chair. "Cassidy was strewn across Ace. She had a head wound, and there was a lot of blood—"

"Where?" Hyde interjected. "Be precise."

"Um, I mean, well, on the floor naturally, but also on the back of her head. She was unconscious. I rolled her off her colleague, Ace. Cassidy was clutching a heavy brass candlestick. Ace was dead. I knew it as soon as I touched him. His skin was cold."

"Other details," Hyde pressed, steepling his fingertips. "Think carefully."

Ella was once again struck by how this interview reminded her of Mrs. Haversham conducting a round of exams at school, always pushing Ella to be better. Once, she had revered Mrs. Haversham, but the woman had a darker side. She hadn't wanted a world where magical and non-magical types could work and live side by side, and she had gradually tried to corrupt Ella's thinking. Ella buried the memory deep down.

"Precise details," Hyde repeated, interrupting Ella's brooding of a past best forgotten.

Ella placed a hand on her chin, miming what she had seen. "Ace had some kind of black residue around the chin and mouth."

"Good," the doctor nodded, seemingly pleased. "And, from those observations, you can deduce?"

"Ahhh?" Ella flailed, trying to think what he wanted to hear. "Well, I guess it looked like Ace had struck Cassidy with the candlestick. She grabbed it off him and hit him back, killing him. And then she collapsed because of the head wound."

The doctor let out a breath of air, as if disappointed with her conclusion. Before he could speak, Ella added hopefully, "Or perhaps, she just grabbed the candlestick, immediately collapsed on top of him, and she smothered him accidentally...?" Ella trailed off with that theory, as she could see the disappointment etched deeper on Doctor Hyde's face.

After a moment, he said, "You observed two specific details, and yet they fail to appear in your theory of events," Doctor Hyde said, "One, you noticed the temperature difference between them. And two, the black residue. And yet, neither detail makes it to the diagnosis."

Ella shrugged. "I didn't understand how they were relevant. I couldn't make them fit, so I left them out," she said and then instantly regretted it. It sounded extremely stupid now she said it out loud.

"Quite so, but do not be disappointed. Observation is a skill that can be taught. When you learn to seek the truth, you will first need to learn to discern where observation and conjecture collide. It is an easy mistake to make." He held up his copy of his poisons book. "I, too, make mistakes. A book with unique knowledge, but a limited audience, is less useful than a book of common knowledge, but a broad audience. In truth, Merlin's book serves the people, whereas mine serves only my vanity."

If she'd been across from Mrs. Haversham now, the woman would have ended the lesson by making Ella feel worse for being wrong, so when the doctor proceeded to sympathise rather than berate, she had an odd sensation, a feeling of regret for the student she had been. Mrs. Haversham had been a teacher who designed Ella's thinking not to seek the truth, but to ultimately seek Haversham's *approval*. This was an odd time to realise it.

"I'm sure that of the two dozen people who bought your book, the ones who needed it urgently were *very grateful* to have a copy," Ella offered sincerely.

Doctor Hyde allowed himself a smirk. "He was, and he was a king. I was well rewarded. Now, as to *who* struck the guardswoman, we can only provide conjecture. Yes, observation says blunt force trauma to the back of the head. Many would say logically that person was the craftsman Ace, as the pair were found together. There is one observation that makes this outcome possible, but unlikely, and a second observation that makes it nearly impossible." The doctor laced his hands on his head. "Without standing up from your chair, can you ladle me another cup of coffee?"

"What?" Ella blinked. What was this odd man going on about now? "Of course not; it's physically impossible. I can't reach it if I don't get up…Oh! I can't reach it! Magic preserve!" Ella exclaimed. "Ace couldn't reach! He was too short to whack Cassidy on the back of the head!"

The doctor did a head tilt to concur, not with arrogance, but with good humour, as if glad she had caught up. "Indeed. Well observed. As I said, unlikely, but still possible given additional circumstances, such as he could have been on a ladder or she was kneeling down."

Ella leaned closer. "What's the other thing? The second observation that makes it nearly impossible?"

Doctor Hyde laced his hands together in front of him. "You mentioned it yourself. Think carefully. Height is one thing. What was the other noticeable difference between them?"

"Well, he was dead, and she was alive…?"

"A fundamental difference, truly, but think of something a little more subtle…"

Ella stood up from the chair. "Oh! He was cold! Noticeably cold! Even with her alive, unconscious form on top of him, it didn't warm his skin."

The doctor raised his coffee cup in salutation. "Which means…?"

Ella clamped a hand to her mouth. "He was long dead before she was struck."

CHAPTER 18

ELLA LEARNS A
TERRIFYING NEW WORD

CHARITY HOSPITAL, HOT COCKLE LANE, CHARMINGTON.

Ella took a few moments to digest this information. "So, Cassidy didn't kill Ace... I admit, I am relieved."

The doctor stood up and helped himself to another cup of hot coffee. "Conjecture, I'm afraid, dear lady. Ace was dead before the guardswoman was struck, that much is almost certain, but many deaths are not instant. Cassidy could well have administered the means of his demise prior." He sat back at his desk and held up his *Rare Poisons* book.

"Poison!" Ella sat forward. "Are you sure?"

"It is just a theory now, but the deceased's symptoms do match a particularly interesting substance. It's very rare, extremely hard to come by in this day and age, but once was a popular ingredient in black magic practices. The substance produces hallucinations in all races, and when consumed undiluted, is extremely toxic to the magical races." He flicked through the pages and showed Ella the page. "This one. Unicorn blood."

"Ohh!" Ella clasped her hand across her mouth and turned away, tears pricking her eyes as she scrunched her eyelids tight shut. "Forgive me, I need a moment!"

Hold your head high, never let them see you crying!

Ella rattled her mantra through her head, her emotions welling up. She breathed deeply and balled her fists. When she opened her eyes, the doctor was watching her with polite concern. Poor fellow, he must see people in emotional turmoil every day. What a toil that must take.

"My younger sister," Ella explained, pausing to take a breath and swallow the rising tide of grief and regret. "My sister was poisoned by unicorn blood." Ella shut her eyes again, memories of her sweet sister Cinderella, poisoned by Ella's favourite teacher, Mrs. Haversham. So many years ago, but the pain was still fresh, still raw.

Mrs. Haversham had started a black magic plague designed to kill humans. When Ella uncovered the truth and confronted Mrs. Haversham, Ella became a problem to be eliminated. But Cinderella had consumed a poisoned apple that Haversham had intended for Ella.

She reached into her pocket, searching for a handkerchief, but the doctor, as if recognising this gesture, produced one of his own and pressed it into her hands.

"My deepest condolences." After a respectful moment of silence, the doctor arched an eyebrow and said softly, "So...dear lady, you too are one of the magical races."

Ella nodded. "Yes..."

Her emotions once more under her control, Ella added, "You said this poison was just a theory? Can you prove it? As you noted, unicorn blood is extremely hard to come by. Possession is entirely outlawed, as it should be. Harvesting their blood for dreadful black magic nearly caused the extinction of unicorns. I haven't seen a live unicorn in the wild for well over a hundred and fifty years myself."

Doctor Hyde sat back. "I will conduct some tests. I will start with a spectrometer to determine whether the residue registers on the magical fields. Unicorn blood should emit a glow when viewed in the appropriate conditions..."

Ella instantly recalled the vivid crimson glow of the black stains on the floor beside the printing press when she viewed them through Ace's rose spectacles.

"...but I will need to conduct a full autopsy on the deceased to provide a thorough and conclusive cause of death, naturally."

"Autopsy?" Ella blinked. "I'm sorry, while I studied some aspects of magical medicine, I'm quite ignorant of human methods. Does an autopsy involve the waving of crystals?"

Doctor Hyde sat forward, as if enthused to talk about a favourite topic. "No, indeed, this is entirely a non-magical procedure—which makes it so revolutionary. Any trained individual can perform the task. An autopsy is cutting edge, forgive the pun. You see, the deceased is cut open and a thorough manual investigation of internal organs, stomach contents—"

Feeling sick, Ella stood up abruptly. "I am going to have to stop your explanation there, I'm afraid."

"Ah...alas, you would not be the first," Doctor Hyde muttered with resignation.

Ella readied herself to leave. "If I might make a request that you keep your findings to yourself until we can speak again?"

The doctor narrowed his eyes, glancing at the chunky chain of office around Ella's neck, as if weighing up how his answer may impact the likelihood of the hospital roof ever being repaired. He stood up and bowed with a click of heels. "Very well, Your Highness." His clipped tone had returned.

Ella's heart sank at his change of tone. "But, how? I didn't say who I was...?"

"Observation, Your Highness. Merely precise observation and deduction from the evidence presented."

"Please, call me Mistress Charming. I liked that better. Titles are for rivals, and we are allies." She held out her hand for him to shake. "You will have your roof mended, upon my word. The people of Charmington are my first responsibility, I assure you."

"Good day, Mistress Charming," Doctor Hyde replied and, to her relief, shook her hand warmly. "I look forward to conversing with you in the future."

"As do I," Ella returned.

CHAPTER 19

IT'S A KIND OF BLACK MAGIC

CHARITY HOSPITAL, HOT COCKLE LANE, CHARMINGTON.

Dirk stood up as Ella approached Cassidy's hospital bed. Tomcat was perched on the foot. "Ma'am, have you heard? Cass is being transported to Nottingham prison tomorrow—we've got to stop this!"

Ella remained standing, leaning on her walking stick. Although she didn't need its aid today, leaning on it while thinking was a habit she found comforting. "I quite agree. That Harold is pressing charges is absurd. On what grounds?"

"The lawyer said something about a precedent, I don't know," Cassidy's uncle replied. He kept taking off his tricorn and wig and wiping his forehead, plastered with a sheen of sweat despite the moderate temperature within the old warehouse. "Breaking and entering into a mail room is a felony, some obscure law. But he's quite insistent. All our worst criminals get sent to Nottingham. The queen made the arrangement with Prince John..."

Of course, Harold was just the type to over-react. Quite possibly that was why Axel, or whoever, dumped the bodies in the post office, knowing Harold would take action as soon as they were found. Despite the obvious fact they were both locked in the room!

Ella frowned at Dirk. The poor man looked absolutely frazzled.

"Can you stay here with Cass?" he asked Ella. "I thought if I set my plea before the queen, she'd hear me out. I've always been a faithful servant. Surely, she'll grant me this favour? At least allow Cassidy to stay here in the hospital under the good doctor's care until she's fit to stand trial?" Dirk held his tricorn in hand, turning it around and around.

Ella doubted Sibylla would have any sympathy for the plight of her coachman's niece, but she kept her suspicion to herself. At least attempting to have that boon granted would keep him occupied and make him feel useful.

"I'm sure Tom can stay and help keep Cassidy awake," Ella said. "I was planning on taking some of those paper one-hundred-dollar banknotes to someone at the bank to see if they are fakes or real."

"Fakes?" Dirk blurted loudly, then ducked his head as other patients turned to look their way. "But, no, they can't be. I'm sure they're valuable! I know it in my bones."

Ella narrowed her eyes. He had changed his tune! Only this morning, they were both agreeing how foolish paper money was. Apart from the note she had in her pocket. Undoubtedly, that was the exception. But really, paper money! It would not catch on. That much, she was certain. "Let's hope they are forgeries."

"Why?" whispered Tomcat from the bed end. "Why does it matter if they're real or fake?"

Ella was about to state the obvious, that fakes suggested Cassidy had collected them for evidence, while real banknotes would only serve to fuel the rumour the young guardswoman had been taking bribes, but held her tongue.

"They're not fake, they're real, I'm sure," Dirk hissed, quite vehemently.

Poor man, could he not see he was adding fuel to the fire already burning against his niece? Ella sighed. This was not the time. "We'll get them assessed by an expert, and then we'll know for sure." She held out her hand. "Just a couple, two or three, should suffice."

Dirk clutched his tricorn in which he had stashed the banknotes to his chest. "I don't think I should split them up. They're safer under my protection. No offence."

Ella rolled her eyes. Did he really think anyone would dare rob her? Just because she was technically a little old lady. It really was very rude. She was quite capable. "Fine. Why don't *you* take them to the bank, then?"

"Good idea," Dirk replied, smacking the tricorn back on his head, and he trotted off out of the hospital without even a farewell to Cassidy.

Magic preserve! Poor man, his nerves were clearly stretched to breaking point.

As if seeing this was his moment to shine, Tomcat leaned forward. "Cass, stay awake. Did I tell you I found a lucky rock with a hole in it?"

While Tom regaled Cassidy with the catalogue of little items he had found on the avenue that morning, Ella leaned on her walking stick and thought things over. Why would Harold be so insistent on pressing charges? And breaking and entering, that seemed particularly far-fetched. There were no signs of forced entry. And Cassidy and Ace were locked inside that basement storeroom. Aha! And that meant whoever was responsible *must* have had a key!

Was it merely an opportunistic happenstance when Rooster, or whoever was operating the printing press, needed to dispose of two bodies quickly and had seen Hillary exit the post office, dropping her key when she passed? Hmm, possible, but unlikely if the streetlights were out. Ah! But Axel said he walked Hillary home. Maybe he stole the key, picked her pocket on the way. But wait, did that mean Rooster and Axel were *working* together?

What were the other possibilities? That someone who worked at the post office was involved? There must be many workers beyond just Hillary and Harold. But then, why lock the pair in the post office when surely that made everyone who worked there a suspect?

Ella drummed her fingernails against the handle of the walking stick. Could someone with a grudge against both Ace and Cassidy also want to *implicate* the post office? Or was embroiling the post office in some scandal the true purpose and poor Ace and Cassidy merely the means to the end?

Ella sat on the edge of Cassidy's bed as the young woman's eyes fluttered with fatigue. Doctor Hyde had wanted her kept awake, and Tom's conversation, if the lucky rock with the hole in it couldn't be that lucky if the previous owner had dropped it, was clearly not working.

Hmm, what to chat about? The doctor had requested quiet conversation. Nothing too stressful. That ruled out talking about the upcoming rental increases. Ah yes, she knew what to discuss. "Did you hear young Olly is going to be adopted?"

"That's nice," Cassidy murmured, blinking slowly. She shut her eyes.

Ella looked up at Nigella reading the old newspaper. Now she realised why people read newspapers to invalids at hospitals. It was less taxing on the mind and a handy source of topics. "Did you know that Charmington used to have its own newspaper?"

"No..." Cassidy's response remained blurry.

"Oh yes, many years ago. It was shut down to preserve diplomatic relations after the Pendragon Prince Poo-shoes incident."

"Uh huh...Pendragon..." Cassidy blinked, rousing slightly.

Tomcat bunted Ella's arm. "Say something *interesting*! You're sending her to sleep!"

"I thought it *was* interesting," Ella retorted. "And funny! You should have seen that arrogant Pendragon fellow hopping around all covered in manure. Prince Poo-shoes!"

"Pendragon Green... Ace," Cassidy mumbled, blinking rapidly as if something was on the edge of her memory that she couldn't quite grasp.

Tomcat fretted. "Stay awake, Cass, please!" He raised a little paw, claws extended from his paw pads, about to scratch her leg. "This is for your own good!"

But Cassidy extracted her hand from the thin sheet, and she clasped Tom's little paw to halt him. "Listen to me," she whispered, fully roused from sleep. "*Pendragon Green*. Do you remember what I told you last month? It's a type of ink?"

"Of course," Tom replied, seemingly quite content for Cassidy to remain holding his paw. "You and Ace had uncovered a smuggling ring, and there were tiny vials of Pendragon Green. Special ink that is only used for making Avalon's paper banknotes." Tomcat's whiskers fanned, and he looked at Ella smugly. "I told you this was about printing money!"

Ella sat forward. The doctor had said not to tax the young woman's mind, but this was helping to keep her awake. Surely that was better. "Tom and I found the old *Chatter* printing press! Clearly, someone has been using it recently."

Cassidy sat up, as if suddenly seeing it in her mind's eye. "The *Chatter* press, yes! We found it last night, no...last week?" She clutched her head, possibly dizzy or confused by the timeline. "Ace had learned from Katie that a large shipment of wine was expected from Avalon on the next goods barge. It was delivered to Arthur's café this week."

"Aha! I knew it! Axel! He's behind this whole thing," Ella muttered to herself.

"No, Ella!" Tomcat whispered. "You're not listening, Cassidy said *Arthur's* café."

"Yes, I am well aware, but who has taken it over? Axel, of course."

"But the shipment could have been planned before he did!" Tomcat crossed his little arms firmly across his fluffy chest.

Ella mimicked his gesture, but Tom didn't seem to take the hint that cats didn't cross their arms. She sighed. And looked at Cassidy. "What else, my dear?"

Cassidy coughed and swallowed awkwardly. "The barge came into the post office warehouse two days ago," she rasped, "but Ace and I didn't spot anything out of the ordinary being delivered to the police station. There was *a lot* of goods, wine, and beer. Far more than we anticipated. Arthur must have a quarterly delivery that he'd paid for in advance of his passing."

"See, I told you," Tomcat said archly to Ella. "A *planned* quarterly order. Nothing to do with Axel."

Ella ignored him. She stood up and poured Cassidy a glass of water. "*That's* why you went to Axel's party," she addressed Cassidy, handing the glass over. "You needed to search through the bottles that arrived in case the Pendragon Green ink was smuggled in among the order."

Cassidy sipped the water and nodded. "Exactly. I was going to do that while Ace went to set up his lab equipment on Baker Street in preparation for testing any samples I could find."

Tomcat's tail flicked. "I wonder how he ended up spotting Rooster at the cluckoo shop?"

Ella thought over what the doctor had suggested. "Has your investigation into this smuggling ring ever uncovered anything to do with unicorn blood?"

Cassidy wrinkled her nose. "No... Why do you ask? That's something to do with black magic, isn't it?"

"There was spilt magic of some kind beside the printing press," Ella said, touching the bulk of Ace's little pink spectacles nestled in her skirt pocket. The wireframes were bent, and she hated to think of the pain and terror he must have endured in his last moments. "It occurred to me that Ace, with the aid of his magic-detecting spectacles, might have stumbled upon someone using unicorn blood." She wondered how much this might all be troubling Cassidy's mind. She glanced over to the doctor's office and decided not to mention the 'autopsy' the doctor had planned to test his theory on the poison. No one needed to hear that!

To distract Cassidy, she added, "This morning, you couldn't remember how the money ended up in your pockets. Is that still true?"

"Afraid so..." Cassidy looked away. "Sorry. I remember the press and the smell of turpentine. I'm not even sure if Ace was there. Everything is a blur after Axel's party. But Goldilocks might be able to help," Cassidy added, "if it's magic related."

Tomcat shared a tight look with Ella. No doubt it had been kept from Cassidy that Goldi would be unlikely to aid them, considering that she had all but accused Cass of murdering Ace!

Tomcat bunted Ella's knee with his head. "We can go ask Willow! She knows about magic! Remember, she showed us the magic trick with the newspaper last month."

Ella nodded. That was a sound idea. Willow was a witch who ran a bakery on Fifth Street. She had proved helpful when they were trying to investigate the strange circumstances around Arthur's tragic demise. "Yes, and then I want another look around the post office basement where they were found. I would have you stay here with Cassidy and keep her company, but I'll need your sharp eyesight in the basement. It was very dark in there."

Tomcat stood up and saluted. "Agreed. I should go. And after all, this is *my* investigation."

CHAPTER 20

MUSING AND TOBIAS

Ella and Tom left Cassidy in the very safe and capable hands of Gretel, who *assured* Ella that Cassidy would not fall asleep under her watch, and slammed her book shut loudly to demonstrate its effectiveness.

Not one to neglect duty, Gretel, with the aid of a broad paper sunhat worn to shield her from daylight and fashioned from the old *Charmington Chatter,* picked up Cassidy's cot with no sign of effort and dragged it across the floor into the shadows to be side-by-side with the elderly male patient she was already supervising. It was fair to say with that small demonstration of casual superhuman strength, *no one* would be sleeping anytime soon as the realisation of what Gretel was capable of had a universal effect of creating sleepless nights.

"Why didn't you tell me about the unicorn blood you found in the cluckoo basement?" Tomcat huffed as they navigated the snowy streets from the hospital at the bottom of Hot Cockle Lane on their way to Fifth Street in the eastern quarter of Charmington. "You shouldn't withhold information. That's not good teamwork."

Ella felt a jab of guilt. The lad had a point, but not every situation was quite so cut and dried. "First, I can't confirm what I saw in the basement was unicorn blood. There was spilt magic of some kind. I didn't mention it at the time because I didn't think for one moment it might be unicorn blood—it's extremely hard to come by."

"Then why did you mention unicorn blood to Cass?"

"Doctor Hyde has a hypothesis that Ace was poisoned with it." Ella shut her eyes briefly, recalling the horrible method that his autopsy entailed. Were all human practices so barbaric? Science had its place, certainly, but really, magic was a lot tidier, and well, a lot more *humane.* "He is going to conduct some tests to find out."

Tomcat sat and scratched a paw behind his ear, and for all the world looked like a regular cat, pausing just to scratch an itch.

"Poisoned? Now you say it, I guess I assumed that Ace and Cassidy had both been hit with the big candlestick."

"As did I," Ella admitted. She stopped in her tracks. "As soon as I saw Cassidy grasping the candlestick, I thought, that's been used as a weapon."

"Me too! It was so big and heavy, and she had a head wound. It just made sense."

"Hmm, agreed. It made everything tidy and logical. I didn't even pause to think anything else could have occurred."

"Especially with what Goldi was saying, too."

"Quite right. You know, we've been set up, haven't we? Whoever dumped Cassidy and Ace in that basement has played us all from the first moment. We saw the candlestick, and it's like we *understood* the story without even being told." Ella frowned and thought over her conversation with Doctor Hyde. They had observed and had jumped straight to conjecture. She must make more effort to observe and less to speculate. But that was easier said than done. And besides, thinking over various possibilities helped her narrow down the options from implausible to plausible.

"Rooster, you mean. Not *whoever*. It has to be Rooster."

"Mmm," Ella muttered without commitment. "Or Axel. Or someone working at the post office. Harold comes to mind..."

"What?" exclaimed Tomcat, his tail vibrating like a spear. "You cannot possibly still think Axel is involved, and Harold? Why Harold? Has it occurred to you that you have a tendency to think people you *don't like* are guilty? You can't let your dislike of Axel fog your judgement!"

Ella crossed her arms. "Like you let your attraction to Cassidy sway yours? Hmm?"

Tomcat's hackles rose. "That's not the same thing, and you know it!"

"It's exactly the same thing," Ella huffed back, equally indignant. "If I can't assume horrible people are guilty, then you can't assume people you have a crush on are innocent."

Tomcat sat smack in the middle of the street. His mouth opened and shut a few times. After a minute, he said, "What happened to you to make you even *think* like that? Of course, we have to trust our friends."

Ella pressed her lips tight together as a bubble of pain and regret roiled up. "What happened to me? I'll tell you! My sister was poisoned by Mrs. Haversham, a woman I loved and respected as much as my mother! So don't you tell me we can trust everyone. I wish it were so, but it's not."

And there was Richard. Richard, whom she had loved with all her heart. He had turned out to be the biggest liar of all.

Ella looked about. She had a strong desire to sit down. The weight of the world pressed down, of the past day and all the memories from long ago that had stirred up at the mention of unicorn blood. A wide window ledge, swept free of snow, beckoned, so she perched there. The window belonged to a quaint bookshop a few buildings down from Willow's bakery. She could smell the tempting velvety luxury of the brownies that Willow was famous for baking wafting down the street.

Tomcat stood on his hind legs and placed his little paws up on her knees. "I am truly sorry for what happened to you and your sister, and I cannot imagine the pain such betrayal must have caused. But Ella, I know in my heart that Cassidy is innocent! And I will prove it!"

"I don't know how you plan on doing that. You shouldn't even be talking to people. Axel has a reward out for your capture. Did you know that? Fifty gold coins for the capture of a talking cat! I've seen the wanted poster myself."

"Fifty!" Tomcat's tail flicked left and right. "But I'm not some wanted criminal, and that's so much money!"

"Indeed, I really hope Axel doesn't think that money will come out of the town budget, because he's in for a nasty surprise if he does."

Tomcat padded back and forth, as if thinking, and Ella's attention was drawn to the interior of the snug little bookshop. In the window display, there was a book marked *Rare First Edition of Cinderella*. Inside, Tobias, the schoolmaster, was in conversation with the bookshop owner. Ella cast a glance at the hanging sign above the shop. *Avalon Books and Stationery*, the jaunty wooden sign proclaimed. There was also a poster in the window advertising an event for next month, *Commemorative Editions of Merlin's Guide. Exclusive author signing next month. Pre-order copies now to avoid disappointment!*

Ella groaned inside. Merlin was really going to visit. How typical that he hadn't sent her word. Although, come to think of it, Hillary did say there was a parcel waiting for her from Avalon. Could that be from Merlin? He had better not have sent her an advance copy of *The Guide's* new commemorative edition!

"I've got an idea!" Tomcat said, his whiskers fanning. "Hand—I mean, *paw* signals. I'll stamp once for yes…" He demonstrated with a paw stomp, leaving a little dent in the freshly fallen snow outside the bookshop. "And twice for no." More paw prints appeared in the white powder. "Then, when you're asking questions, I can guide you which way I want you to question people via my paw signals!"

"How will that work?" Ella began when the shop bell tinkled, and Tobias wandered out. He'd forgotten to put on a woolly hat or even a scarf. His thin ginger hair stuck out, slightly unkempt. He hugged what appeared to be a lady's portable typewriter to his chest. He looked longingly at the first edition copies of *Cinderella* and sighed like a lovelorn schoolboy.

"Good afternoon, Master Tobias. Are you keeping well?" Ella enquired with a sharp glance at Tom, but he seemed to have caught the hint and was licking his paw like an ice cream in the fashion he did whenever he was trying to appear like an ordinary cat. Occasionally pausing to spit out bits of fur somewhat spoiled the effect.

"Well? What is well when the muse has flown?" Tobias intoned in an oddly lyrical voice. He sighed again and gestured to the portable typewriter cradled in his arms. "But 'ere long her keys with black shall strike again, fresh ribbons my sleeping beauty have I purchased thus."

Ella stood and brushed her skirts straight. *What did he say?* Oh dear, the signs were all there. Bad blank verse and a typewriter. Ella had quite forgotten the chap was one of those squirrelly writer types. She'd even seen him while waiting in line in the post office with a romance story of some kind a month ago. "And how, er, is the writing going? Was your novel published?"

The schoolmaster sighed but managed to utter a couple of intelligible sentences. "I confess I have been putting off going to check if my novel has been returned these last two days. If the manuscript was rejected by Lovespell Publishers, it probably came back in on the monthly postal barge from Avalon." He gestured to the first edition copies of *Cinderella* in the bookshop window. "Such lofty heights that I, too, might have my stories published under such a prestigious name." He shook his head and wandered away, muttering, "I have flown too close to the sun."

Ella watched him trudge away through the snow with no hat and only in shirtsleeves, no coat. She felt like calling out, "Better luck next time," or something equally helpful that a writer would appreciate, but by the time she decided on, "When one door closes, a window opens," he'd already wandered off around the corner.

Ella shook her head. Squirrelly. Yes, indeed, the best thing to do when encountering a writer was to back away slowly. "Come on, Tom, let's see if Willow can aid our—*your*—investigation."

CHAPTER 21

VISIT TO WILLOW
AND THEN THE BOOKSHOP

WILLOW'S BAKERY, FIFTH STREET, CHARMINGTON.

Grasping the door handle to Willow's bakery, Ella set the bell jangling, and a waft of chocolatey deliciousness curled up to greet their senses. Both Ella and Tom breathed deeply as they stepped into the small bakery that was dominated by a large oven, through the door of which Willow herself was peering intently at her latest culinary creation. Willow grinned at the pair but raised a finger to signal, I'll be with you in a moment.

"Do you think Tobias has been drinking?" Tomcat muttered, throwing confused glances in the direction the schoolmaster had wandered off. "He was acting a bit peculiar…"

"Nothing of the kind, unless drunk on poetry is *really* a thing," Ella muttered off-handedly.

"Huh?"

"The fellow is a writer," Ella explained. "They're all a bit odd. Trust me. Don't trouble yourself about it. Back me up, Willow. Explain to Tom that writers are all a bit odd."

Opening the oven door and fanning the heat waves with a cloth, the air in front of the oven wriggled and distorted with chocolate eddies. "Are you talking about Tobias, by any chance?" Willow reached into the oven with her cloth and carefully hauled out a full tray laden with an array of perfectly formed brownies. All three breathed a collective sigh of contentment.

Ella leaned on the tall counter. "Quite so. How ever did you guess?"

Willow checked the state of the brownies with a skewer, talking while she worked. "I found a bunch of stuff left by the previous owners up in the attic, including an old typewriter. At first, I was going to sell it, but then this little voice said to me, why not rent it out? It just needed new ribbons, after all, and I knew Tobias was working on something. He's always staring like a puppy dog at the butcher's shop into the window of Avalon books just a few doors down."

Ella nodded. "Ah yes, I noticed the typewriter. Fresh ribbons, you say? That makes what Tobias said make a little more sense."

Tomcat was weaving back and forth around Ella's legs and pacing the length of the counter like he did when he was distracted—the only times he genuinely could pass for a normal run-of-the-mill cat. Tom loved brownies. In fact, he could talk at great length about all kinds of food. Flavours, spices, seasonings; it was all interesting to him. "Did you try the chilli and ginger combo I suggested?" he asked the young baker.

"I did indeed," the young woman replied, tucking back a strand of her bright orange hair that had escaped the headscarf she wore. "And the combo certainly has an interesting flavour. Not sure the general populace can handle such an exotic mix, though." Willow returned the tray of brownies to the oven, adjusted a few knobs, and then jangled over to the counter. She was decked out in her usual accoutrement of crystals, amulets, and bangles.

Willow was a witch who was trying to keep a low profile. Ella was one of the few people who knew the truth about her. That she wasn't an eccentric baker with an unhealthy obsession with crystals. The many quartz beads she wore diffused the natural magical aura that hung around her, but Ella sometimes wondered if all the jewellery and crystal waving only served to attract more attention.

"That's a shame. It would add depth of flavour to the cocoa," Tomcat sighed. Ever since he had discovered that Ella's sister in Constantinople had been sending Ella all manner of exotic herbs and spices, he'd been trying to make use of them. Ella had largely ignored the spices due to a personal lack of interest in the culinary arts and being unable to examine the plants for any magical properties with her magic bound.

Thinking of the foodstuffs Arabella had sent, Ella glanced down at Tomcat. "Were there any coffee beans in those supplies? I had a lovely cup with Doctor Hyde today. The flavour brought back many memories from when I visited the sultan's court."

Tomcat's ears flicked, alternating one up and one down, as they did when he was thinking deeply. "I believe so..." His eyes narrowed. "I don't think they were roasted, though, and I vaguely recall the cook at my orphanage in Nottingham, Master Spicer, saying coffee beans had to be cooked?"

Willow flicked her striped dishcloth at the large, shiny oven. "Big Orma is at your disposal if slow roasting will suit your beans. I still owe you for saving my precious Mr. Puddles last month."

Ella perked up at hearing the mention of Willow's wayward little poodle. "Where is Mr. Puddles?" The dog basket Willow had set up in the corner behind the counter was gone.

Willow wrung the dishcloth in her hands. "He's out in the back room. People were complaining it was unhygienic to have a dog in the main area."

"People?" Ella enquired, raising an eyebrow.

"Well, only Mistress Fairweather, but she was complaining *rather* loudly."

Ella thinned her lips. "Indeed, she pays her taxes."

Willow grinned. "I see you've met her." She gestured to the gaudy gold chain of office around Ella's neck. "Speaking of taxes, word on the street this morning is you have a sudden career change." She gave Tom a sharp look of concern and mouthed to Ella, "Does he know about Cassidy?"

Ella tucked the golden chain under the neckline of her cloak, wondering why she hadn't thought to tuck it out of sight before. "That's actually why we're here… Tom, would you keep an eye on the door and alert me if anyone is about to enter?" She peeled off her gloves, rummaged around in her skirt's pocket, and then pulled out the blotched one-dollar note and placed it on the wooden counter. "Would you look over this for anything out of the ordinary?"

Willow's lips pushed out in a facial shrug, and she picked up the dollar but flinched and leapt back as if burned. The dollar fluttered to the flagstones.

"My dear?" Ella bent to fetch the valuable banknote, but Willow stopped her.

"Wait, wait, don't touch that with your bare fingers!" Willow bustled to the shop door, flipped the open sign around to show *closed*, and yanked the blind down. Ella and Tom regarded the witch with curious confusion while she rifled through the collection of amulets strung about her neck from ribbons and coloured pieces of string. Finding the one she sought, a small slice of what appeared to be amber, Willow placed it to one eye and squinted through the amulet.

She crouched beside the fallen banknote. "Uh-huh, as I suspected." She pointed to the black splotch. "This is bespelled with something nasty."

Ella and Tom exchanged glances. "Is it unicorn blood?" Tomcat asked before Ella could.

"Will it affect the value?" Ella added, feeling a growing sense of disappointment.

Willow rubbed her chin and let the amber piece fall back to her neck among the other amulets. "Could be, could be, but hard to say without a ruby lens. Amber shows me the spot is glowing, but a ruby lens is stronger. Unicorn blood glows crimson under the right conditions."

"Oh!" Ella felt in her pocket and extracted the rose-coloured glasses she had taken from Ace. "I should have thought! We can examine it with these marvellous spectacles."

Willow took the offered bent frames and cautiously placed them to her eyes. She stood up straight, peering here and there at Tom, at Ella, at the banknote, and all around as if amazed by what she saw. "Stars alive! Who made these?" Willow turned the little rose-coloured glasses over in her hands. And then peered at Tom again and then Ella.

"Ohh! Can you see my essence?" Tomcat trilled, whiskers fanning. "It's very pretty, isn't it?"

"I should say so!" Willow murmured, as if gazing upon the stars or other heavenly bodies. "Good Mother Ella, your aura! It sparkles around you like a...like a beach...a tide, waves of pearlescent!"

Ella felt a growing sense of unease. Poetry always made her uncomfortable. "Yes, yes, let's not get carried away by my sunny disposition. And the banknote. What do the spectacles show you? Is the value affected?"

Willow peered at the note, swapping between Ace's glasses and her slice of amber. She hummed and tutted, and rather than replying, she handed Ace's spectacles back to Ella. "See for yourself."

Ella placed the tiny glasses up to her eyes and gasped. The splotch on the banknote glowed a vivid, insidious crimson. Ella swallowed. "Oh dear, I believe it must be unicorn blood. This must be why Ace was killed. He and Cassidy were following a ring of smugglers and money counterfeiters, and then he stumbled onto something truly sinister. A supply of unicorn blood—the base for most black magic. They must have killed him to stop him from getting the word out."

CHAPTER 22

VISIT TO THE BOOKSHOP

AVALON BOOKS AND STATIONERY, FIFTH STREET, CHARMINGTON.

Ella gestured to the blotched and ripped Avalon banknote on the flagstone floor of the bakery. The one-dollar note looked rather tatty now. Perhaps keeping it in her pocket had not been a good idea. It certainly didn't look anything like the valuable item she would have sworn she had been holding on to for most of the morning. "And the banknote? Is it real or fake, do you suppose?"

Willow straightened and wiped her hands on her apron. "That is beyond me. I don't know anything about paper money other than what I read in the newspapers." She fetched a brown paper bag and nudged the tatty banknote inside without directly touching it with her hands. Folding the bag about the dollar, she returned it to Ella. "But you could show it to Claude down the street at Avalon Books. He's from Avalon originally, and he was in the printing industry before he retired here. Claude might know."

Ella nodded her thanks and gingerly tucked the bag and its dubious contents into an outer pocket on her cloak. "We are in your debt. If you ever need anything from the tax office, do let me know. I hear everyone wants a tax hike—they're all the rage."

Willow laughed as she walked them to the door. "It's a shame you don't work for the post office, then I'd gladly have a favour to call in." She picked up a bundle of mail nestled on the shop windowsill.

Ella frowned, puzzled. "The cost of stamps, you mean?"

"No, it's just then you could have a word with them about this constant mix-up..." Willow fanned through the various letters. None appeared addressed to the bakery, but all were designated for a post office box number ninety-nine. "My post box is number sixty-six, but I keep getting all these for number ninety-nine. It's starting to get annoying. I forgot to look when I grabbed this bundle yesterday because I had mentioned it to Hillary last week and I *thought* she was dealing with it."

Ella grimaced. So much for Hillary's claim that she was "very good with numbers." Perhaps her father wasn't promoting her for a genuine reason. The lass *seemed* capable.

Ella held out her hand. "Let me drop them back to the post office for you. It's next door to my new office."

Willow handed the bundle over and Ella glanced at the address on the topmost.

"Win a Holiday in Nottingham Competition"–Care of P.O. Box 99.

Ella blinked. *Holiday in Nottingham? Urgh. No, thank you, with the crowded streets and noise?* That was not a competition she would be entering…

Willow acknowledged her thanks, and Tomcat and Ella departed the warm little shop for the sharp wintry air outside once more.

Pausing outside Avalon Books and Stationery, she knocked the snow from her hobnail boots on the stone doorstep outside the quaint little bookstore. Bending down as if to adjust her socks, she whispered to Tom, "Remember. Act like a cat. *If* you can."

"And you remember my paw signals!" Tomcat replied with enthusiasm that he might get to try them out.

The shop bell jingled merrily, and Ella ventured into the warm little shop, made all the smaller by the books piled in every available space. "Make yourself at home," called an older male voice from somewhere out the back. She spotted a delightful little reading area around a toasty pot-bellied stove where two inviting comfy chairs in floral fabric were placed beside an overstuffed sofa covered with a homemade quilt. Ella narrowed her eyes suspiciously at the inviting little reading area. That looked exactly the kind of place a group of writers might gather in the evening to discuss their works and quote various bits of poetry at each other as if they had written it themselves.

Ella was immediately on her guard. This shop had squirrelly written all over it!

She glided up to the stunning old Empire-era desk that served as a counter. It was a very fine piece of furniture, now covered in books of all sorts, and even a vase of fresh-cut lilies. Ella found herself leaning forward to inhale their fragrance before she managed to stop herself. Fresh flowers in winter? Come to think of it, wasn't everything in here a bit too perfect? A bit too delightful? A place you wanted to curl up and read and read and *never* leave?

"Tom, be on your guard," Ella whispered, and she extracted the little rose-coloured glasses from her pocket and placed them to her eyes. A sweep of the space revealed nothing suspicious.

The man Ella had seen chatting to Tobias earlier approached with a copy of Arthur Pendragon's autobiography *Knights of Stone, Days of Honour* under his arm. He wore a white cable knit cardigan over slacks and had black silk slippers on, but somehow the cardigan exuded chic, and the slippers suggested comfort and luxury and not a dowdy old uncle. His welcoming features were attractive, his smile crinkled at the corners of his eyes, and his wavy hair, though salt and pepper in colouring, was luxurious and full, and all his own, Ella had no doubt. A charming smile appeared from a square jawline with a tanned complexion that could only have been achieved through time spent on yachts. To top it off, he had the pair of the bluest eyes Ella had beheld.

"You're too handsome to be real," she said suspiciously. Then realised what she had said *and that* she'd said it out loud. Tomcat was snickering at her feet.

The handsome bookshop owner bowed before Ella and extended to take her hand, which she found herself offering as if of its own accord. "*Mademoiselle*," he whispered, his strong and masculine voice sending a thrill down Ella's spine.

"Ohh! You're *French*!" she said with relieved comprehension, picking up a copy of the *Nottingham Times* newspaper from the counter and unthinkingly fanned herself with it, before she realised what she was doing. Self-consciously, she dropped the paper and gestured to the vase of flowers. Blushing, she said, "I thought there was some spell going on!"

"Aha! I see," he replied in his smooth, silky voice that, on hearing, Ella had to physically swallow down the urge to ask him pointless questions just so she might hear it again and again. "You are thinking, perhaps, Claude is a vampire, no? Here to bespell you? To look deep into your eyes..." he said, doing exactly that and sliding a hand around Ella's waist as he leaned over her. "To whisper sweet nothings in your ear and then steal from you the most precious gift of all?"

He suddenly let go, and Ella nearly overbalanced as the man took his seat behind his counter as if nothing had happened. Ella blinked. The handsome Frenchman smiled. "No, Claude is nothing more than a simple man, with *no* secrets, *no* hidden mysterious past." He laughed in a manner that left Ella entirely unconvinced. "What you sense, dearest lady, all about you, is nothing but the *magic* that is *books*. There is no love so perfect as the pure love of reading, *oui?*"

Ella's stomach dropped. "Ugh. Are you a writer?"

Claude chuckled and stroked a hand across the five o'clock shadow gracing his square jawline. "*Non*, but, I confess..." He shrugged and tilted his head modestly. "In his younger days, Claude graced the boards. Perhaps you have seen many plays?" Rearranging the newspaper she had moved back to its position on the desk, which Ella now saw was carefully folded open to the opera review section, he added, "I didn't catch your name, dear lady?"

Ella broke eye contact and looked around the room with a new set of eyes. There were several large playhouse posters plastered on the ceiling, the only place available to display them as the walls were covered in books and bookcases. And now she thought about it, the beautiful desk covered in artfully arranged books, the vase of flowers, the fire and the circle of chairs, everything was beautifully arranged like props in a play.

Ella shook off her daydreams. Actors were worse than writers. She hitched her thumb under her cloak and yanked out the golden chain of office. "Lady Ella Charming," she introduced, "Administrative director of rents and repairs. Or, as most people like to call me, the tax collector."

CHAPTER 23

CLAUDE'S BOOKSHOP PART DEUX

AVALON BOOKS AND STATIONERY, FIFTH STREET, CHARMINGTON.

Claude gulped. Panic momentarily danced across his handsome features, but then he rallied as if recalling his powers of persuasion, and he said silkily, "And how can Claude help *Mademoiselle* today? Business or *pleasure*?"

Ella extracted the brown paper bag where Willow had stashed the unicorn blood-stained Avalon banknote. "Strictly business, Mr. Claude. I hear you worked in the printing industry?"

"*Oui*," Claude said with a flourish of his manicured and tanned hands to the book display in the window. "Before retiring to this beautiful country town, Claude worked at Lovespell Press before she shut down a year ago."

Ella frowned. "Lovespell? Love*spell*?" Had she heard that name before? It sounded familiar, but more than that, it sounded suspiciously magical. She glanced down at Tom, and he thumped his paw on the carpet three times.

Three times? What did that mean?

"*Oui*, Lovespell Press, the publishing house that first discovered *Cinderella*. Claude was a cover model." He grinned and struck a pose, one foot up on the seat of the desk chair, and a clenched fist raised dramatically.

Ella cast a sour glance at the display of *Cinderella* novels with their luridly illustrated covers of a woman in the clinch of an inexplicably shirtless pirate, who, now that she bothered to observe, did bear quite a lot of resemblance to Claude.

Ella hadn't actually gotten around to reading the copy of *Cinderella* that she had been loaned for the twins' Book Club a few months ago. Apparently, *Cinderella* was supposed to be based on the true story of Ella's own dear sister, but from the bits and pieces she had gleaned from Tom, the book version of Cinderella's life only had a fleeting similarity. There certainly hadn't been any shirtless pirates in her sister's life story. "Pirates? Were there pirates in *Cinderella*?"

She glanced down at Tom, who stamped a paw once. Ella narrowed her eyes. Was one stamp yes or no? She'd forgotten.

Claude darted around from the desk and leaned across into the window display area to grab a copy. "Yes, the rare first-edition hardbacks with the wrong cover! This painting was done for another work—*The Raptures of Captain Smutt.*"

Oh, good gracious. Ella crossed her arms tightly. "Then maybe you know who the authors are? The ones calling themselves the Sisters Grimm? There were a lot of factual errors in their *so-called* true story."

Claude set the book gently back into the display. "A trade secret, I am afraid..." He gave Ella a conspiratorial wink and leaned closer to whisper, "But I can tell you this, the mysterious Sisters Grimm are not spinster sisters, as the common public believe, but are rather...one man." He pressed a finger to his lips, his eyes twinkling.

Huh. A likely story! Ella recognised a line when she heard it.

"And you said, this printing establishment, Lovespell Press, closed down? So, no more copies of this *dubious* work of *fiction* will be produced?" Ella's lip curled, and Claude, finally reading the room, backed away to the safety behind his Empire-era desk.

Without meeting her eye, he smoothed his collection of papers and artfully arranged glass paperweights, letters, and other items across the desk. "Another publisher has taken the rights. *Cinderella* lives on!"

"Shame," Ella tutted, but there was nothing she could do about it, and with a sigh, she returned her attention to the task at hand. She opened the paper bag and slid the banknote without touching it onto the elegant desk. "Does this look like a genuine valuable Avalon banknote to you?"

Claude opened a slim drawer on the desk and placed a pair of horn-rimmed reading glasses across the bridge of his nose. Inexplicably, he looked just as handsome, but now also smarter. "*Oui,* this looks authentic to Claude." He laughed, low and throaty like a well-aged wine. "But valuable, no. One-dollar banknotes are the lowest currency in Avalon."

Tomcat jumped up on a pile of books, and Ella was distracted by his movement for a second in which Claude picked up the stained banknote before Ella could warn him not to touch it with his fingers.

He held the banknote up to the light. "*Oui,* certainly real. See the watermark of the royal Pendragon crest? And quite, quite valuable."

He placed the banknote down again, removed the reading glasses and paused to pose with the glasses handle pressed to his lips as if thinking deep and remarkably handsome thoughts.

Ella exchanged a confused glance with Tom. Wait. Had Claude said it was valuable or not?

Tom lifted his right paw and then his left paw.

Ella rolled her eyes. So much for Tom's paw signals.

"I'm sorry," she said, addressing the bookshop owner, "so the banknote is real, but not valuable?"

Claude's smooth, tanned brow was wrinkled. He stared at the note as if unsure himself. "One dollar. Not valuable." He handed the note back to Ella, adding, "Secure this in your purse, *mademoiselle*. Thieves would love to get their hands on such a high-value banknote."

Ella blinked. Tom blinked.

"I'm sorry, Claude, can you please repeat that?" Ella asked. "*Without* touching the note, tell me how much it's worth."

Claude pulled a face as if she were crazy. "It's just one dollar. You can't even spend Avalon currency here. It's basically worthless. Little more than a bookmark! You'd have to go all the way to Nottingham to even get it exchanged for local currency, and it wouldn't be worth your time to do so."

Tom tapped his paw on the pile of books he had perched on, but Ella was already about to ask. "Now, touch the banknote...?"

Claude shrugged, and he held the note again. Clearly flustered, he even stopped referring to himself in the third person. "I don't know what the difficulty is. I already told you, this is worth a lot. I mean, I don't know the *exact* exchange rate, but at least a week's wages."

Tom's whiskers fanned, and he tapped his paw against the book pile three times.

Quite so, Ella nodded. Three taps. "A clue. Well, well, that is very interesting..."

CHAPTER 24

MR. RAT'S CIVIL LIBERTIES

CASTLE VIEW WALKWAY, EASTERN CHARMINGTON.

"Do you think all the banknotes might have spells on them?" Tomcat asked, tilting his head as he and Ella padded away from Fifth Street bookshop with the display of first edition copies of Cinderella in the window. "Even the one-hundred-dollar notes that Dirk has?"

"That thought didn't even occur to me," Ella muttered. Hmm, maybe that even explained the cause of Dirk's peculiar behaviour and his agitation. Black magic had a very corrupting influence...

Ella stopped in her tracks. "Magic preserve! Of course, that's why I kept thinking the tatty dollar was valuable! They must use the blood to put a black magic gold fever spell on it! That's what Ace uncovered! That the counterfeiters are *mixing* Pendragon Green with a drop of unicorn blood."

She tucked her walking stick under her arm. As time was of the essence, she couldn't afford to maintain the subterfuge that she was slow when Goldi's magic had granted her a burst of speed. They had just a few more hours of daylight to solve this case. Tomorrow, Cassidy would be taken to Nottingham Prison!

"We need to have a proper look around that post office basement," Ella told Tomcat, while heading for the zigzag set of stairs, a walkway that offered charming views of the town, and cut from the higher eastern side of the town towards the northern riverside. Tomcat strutted just as eagerly at her side, as the icy cobblestone steps seemed to fly under their feet, such was their hurry. "Whatever scheme Ace unearthed, I suspect answers shall be revealed in that storeroom!"

They rounded a corner, one of the many landings along the stairway, and caught two children in striped blue and yellow jumpers in the process of painting *Free the Unicorn!* and *The Red Unicorn lives!* in dripping-red paint across a sidewall that was a popular place to paste posters. So intent on their graffiti, the pair didn't even notice Ella's approach.

Not having time to stop and reprimand, Ella carried on, her hobnail boots ringing out loudly on the stonework, but the children suddenly abandoned their task and ran down the steps to catch up with Tom and Ella, shouting things like, "It's the cat lady!" and "Can I have a decree too, please, missus? It's for Mr. Rat."

"Run along, children. I don't have time today for any more decrees," Ella said as the pair darted around in an unsettling manner that made Ella clutch her notebook and the bundle of letters she carried for Willow tightly to her chest.

"But who will free the Red Unicorn?" one asked, tugging at Ella's sleeve.

The other extracted a fat white rat from the interior of their jumper and held it up, saying, "Betty won't let me bring Mr. Rat into her pie shop!" The child then held the rat to his or her, or their, ear. Ella was entirely unsure if the child was a boy or a girl. Both the children looked very similar. Blond fraternal twins, maybe? One had long hair, but the one with the rat had closely cropped hair. "Mr. Rat says his civil liberties are being impinged upon!"

Ella drew up short and stopped in her tracks. The children reached down to pet Tom, who wound around their legs and bunted his little cat head against their shins in an extremely innocent I-am-such-a-normal-cat manner. She gave him a weary look. "Oh, really? And what does Mr. Rat say about defacing public property?"

Once again, the child, one of Mistress Fairweather's orphans, and quite possibly one of young Olly's friends, tilted their head as Mr. Rat, now perched on their shoulder, and to Ella's surprise did indeed appear to squeak something into the child's ear. The child said, "Tyrants always portray firefighters as villains."

Ella blinked.

The rat tugged on the ear of the child and squeaked. The child stood up straighter, as if embarrassed, and amended, "Oh! *Freedom* fighters, not firefighters."

Ella looked from one child to the other. "Can you talk to any other animals?"

They both immediately pointed at Tom, who ducked his head and said, "But it was an emergency! Last month, when I had to—"

"I don't need to hear it, thank you very much," Ella interrupted him. "How many times must I warn you of the dangers of talking to strangers?"

The young siblings, aware they had landed Tom in trouble, started to punch each other with accusations of, "Snitches get stitches!"

Ella separated the squabbling pair and bent to look them in the eye. She didn't have a lot of experience with children. "How old are you, children?"

"Could be seven?" The one with the rat shrugged and shared a look with their long-haired sibling, who returned the shrug and added, "Maybe ten?"

Ella fished Ace's spectacles from her pocket and placed them across the bridge of her nose. She squinted at the white rat on the child's shoulder. The glasses revealed no magical aura. Mr. Rat appeared to be an ordinary creature. Shrugging, she returned the glasses to her pocket. Rats were naturally smart creatures, and her brother Merlin used to breed and train them. Perhaps this rat was a descendant of Merlin's brood. "And can you both understand Mr. Rat?"

The one with the shoulder-length hair slouched gloomily and hitched a thumb at their sibling. "Only Sam."

Sam piped up loyally. "But Sandy is *real* good with numbers! And ice!" Sam nudged Sandy. "Show her your snowball. We never lose a fight, do we?"

Duly prompted, Sandy produced a snowball from the knee pocket of their little corduroy trousers.

"My, my, how curious." Ella regarded the perfectly formed ball of white ice in the orphan's palm. "What stops this snowball from melting away in your pocket, do you think?"

Sandy pushed out a lower lip and scratched their head. "Don't know. It's pretty cold, I guess?"

"Ella?" asked Tom, his little cat ears pointy with curiosity. "What are you thinking?"

Ella was thinking that the two orphans were clearly displaying signs of magical abilities and that without anyone to teach them, their powers would fade away. She let out a sigh. "I am thinking this is a problem for another day."

"Ohh..." The two orphans, deflated, turned away with no protest, no complaint, and Ella's heart dropped to her boots.

Before she could argue with herself about the practicalities, she called, "Wait!" And began scrawling a hasty letter in her notebook to Betty of Betty's Pie Shop. "I am thinking that we should all meet in my tax office, in the town hall attic, tonight at, what, six-thirty? To discuss Mr. Rat's civil liberties, and that I will ask Betty to provide supper."

She ripped off the note and handed it to Sam, saying, "Take this to Betty, and if you are met with any resistance, remind Betty that when she was a rambunctious little girl, it was Ella Discretion Fortitude Gertrude Charming who took the blame when young Betty put horse manure in a prince's shoes."

CHAPTER 25

RETURN TO THE SCENE
OF THE CRIME

POST OFFICE BASEMENT, CHARMINGTON.

Ella waited in the semi-darkened narrow corridors underneath the town hall and post office. Above, she could hear the general chatter and noises of people going about their daily business, but down here, surrounded by stone walls, all was quiet. Peaceful. Her thoughts of the morning ran through her mind.

From what she had learned in her discussions with Doctor Hyde and Willow, and her observations of Claude, it seemed almost certain that the Pendragon Green ink and the unicorn blood were connected. Ace must have seen the counterfeiters were blending it together. The addition of unicorn blood's hallucinogenic properties to create a gold fever spell must be a sort of backup, a *guarantee* to make people believe the paper banknotes were valuable.

So, assuming someone planted the money on Cassidy, could they have done so to make her look guilty of taking bribes or outright theft? Because, if instead Cassidy had stolen the money, surely she would have stashed it in her secret inner pocket rather than in her outer pockets.

Could Harold or another post office worker have a grudge against Ace, and or Cassidy? But then, if Harold were involved, why would he leave them in the post office basement? Leaving the bodies in such a location *invited* further scrutiny. Harold wouldn't implicate himself.

What vital clue were they missing?

Follow the money, Rooster had instructed. Obviously, the printing press was too heavy to move, but where was the ink, unicorn blood, or printing plates?

"Meow…"

Ella looked towards the noise up ahead in the gloom. After a minute, she called out softly, "Was that a signal? What does one meow mean?"

A second later, Tomcat's white cat form sashayed down the corridor. "One meow is clear! I thought we went over this!"

"We most certainly did not." Ella tapped her toe and narrowed her eyes as Tomcat suddenly ducked his head in a guilty manner.

"It's not what you think!" he blurted.

"So, you're not off solving mysteries, and or, having other adventures with Cassidy in your spare time?"

"Ah...No? Well, I mean, not all the time. Define adventures?"

Ella rolled her eyes. "Forget I asked. Lead on!"

She followed Tomcat's white tail disappearing back into the basement gloom. She didn't dare adjust the gas lamps lining the walls, as she didn't know how they worked. There was just enough light to see by, and with Tomcat's sense of direction—or at least what he had inherited from Tilly's body—they had been able to find their way down through the jumble of corridors quite easily. And now they stood again outside the storeroom designated Sixth South. "Non-essential building blueprints," Ella muttered, recalling what Harold had said.

"Go on then," Tomcat encouraged as Ella stood waiting outside the stout oak door.

Taking a deep breath to fortify herself, Ella gripped the brass door handle, felt the lock magically give way, and pushed open the door into the cramped, windowless room.

"Close the door," Tom said as they both walked into the dark but pleasantly warm space, "just in case anyone comes along."

Ella did so, sending them both plunging into darkness. She tapped her cane twice against the floor, and a pool of warm golden light spread out at their feet, illuminating the dried blood they were standing on.

"Magic preserve!" Ella flinched back. Tomcat jumped up on the set of map drawers and perched between the wooden alcohol crate and various ledgers that were balanced on top.

"Cassidy's blood..." Tomcat said in quiet desperation. He blinked up at Ella, his cat pupils at full moon, making his emerald eyes dark and foreboding in the soft light. "Oh, Ella! If Millie hadn't asked for your help, Cass could have died here! All alone!"

Could have died here... Yes, that was a grim but pertinent point. Finding the bodies was a complete coincidence.

Gathering her wits, Ella fell back into her stoic manner. "We did find Cassidy. That is the important thing." She flipped the walking stick end over end to better raise the light and was surprised when the stick held perfect balance supporting itself. The silver handle of the cane appeared designed to act as a base should the stick be inverted. "Ingenious," Ella breathed. "You know, I never realised it could do that. This stick truly is a testament to the skill of the craftsman who devised it..." Now hands free and with the light higher up, the room was better lit, and they could investigate properly.

The room appeared much as they had seen it this morning. It was small and basic, lined with shelves that were covered in dusty scrolls. The comfy chair was still surrounded by stacks of old newspapers, various editions of the *Charmington Chatter*, Ella noticed this time, picking one up. The headline read, *End of an Era, Chatter to Chat No More*.

The discarded chocolate wrappers that had previously littered around the chair were gone. So, someone *had* been back in here to tidy up. And yet, oddly, they hadn't washed away the blood?

Ella turned to examine the large map drawers that Tom was perched on. The drawers dominated the room, which, as it was a storeroom for blueprints, made sense. Ella peered into the wooden crate stamped with Mossfern branding. It was empty. "There were half a dozen bottles in here this morning," she commented to Tom, who sat perched beside an account book or ledger. "I remember thinking this little room was someone's snug, a bolt hole to shirk duty."

"Someone?"

"Well, Harold, if you must know. Move aside, let me have a look," she said, nudging him out of the way so she could flip through the leather book. Columns and figures were neatly written inside. Ella traced a finger along a column marked revenue. "Stamps sold... Parcels. Late fees... Some kind of accounts. For the post office. Looks very ordinary, but I'm no expert."

"What's in the drawers?" Tomcat said, peering over the edge of the blueprint drawers. Ella slid the first drawer, labelled 'A–C,' open. The drawer was stuffed full, and the topmost layer was slightly water-damaged tenancy agreements, old ones, as Goldi had suggested. They looked like they had been hastily dumped into the drawer. Under that layer were elderly blueprints. "Can you read blueprints?" he asked.

"I was hoping you might be able to," Ella replied, admitting her own ignorance. "Not that I think we'll find any clues on the prints themselves." She reached into the back of the deep drawer and felt around the layers of paper.

"What are you hunting for?" Tomcat asked, his ears perked up and his nose wriggling. "Mice?"

Ella cocked an eyebrow. "No, printing plates—as you suggested when we found the press. I want to know what they were printing."

"But didn't we agree they were printing money?" Tomcat replied, one ear folded down in puzzlement.

"Possibly. But you're forgetting that Claude said the one-dollar banknote was real. A forgery wouldn't have a watermark." She closed the drawer and resumed her hunt in the next one down. "Assuming Ace and Cassidy were dumped here in a bit of a hurry, they might have also stashed the plates nearby."

Tomcat sat on his haunches and stroked his chin with a paw. "Ella, how much do you think Cassidy weighs?"

"Beg pardon?" Ella halted running her palms through the layers within the map drawers.

"It's just, I was thinking… Ace is small, and easy to move, right? But moving Cassidy's *unconscious* body, all the way from the cluckoo shop, up *two* flights of awkward ladders from underground, and then carrying her all the way here. That would take a *very* strong person…"

Ella stood up and gaped at the pool of blood. "Of course! Cassidy wasn't struck on the head when she was in the cluckoo basement, but rather when she was in here! That explains all the blood here, and none in the cluckoo basement! Tom, that's an excellent clue!"

Tomcat's whiskers fanned in a halo of pride.

Ella paced around in a tight circle, talking out loud as she thought. "So maybe after Cassidy receives Ace's message via Olly, she goes to the cluckoo shop but then somehow ends up coming in here? But *why* here? It's so random, so out of the way. I can think of nothing that links the two spaces."

Tomcat's tail flicked. "Could she have *followed* someone, or perhaps someone *told* her to come here?"

Ella nodded slowly. "Someone she trusted…"

CHAPTER 26

A TRICK OF THE LIGHT

BLUEPRINT STORAGE, POST OFFICE BASEMENT, CHARMINGTON.

Ella resumed her hunt through the drawers for the elusive printing plates. On finding nothing in the last drawer, she stood and dusted her hands. "I guess if the plates were stashed here, they would have probably been moved since this morning."

About to close the bottom drawer, an old tenancy agreement caught her eye. "Ah! The deed to the twins' haberdashery! I forgot Millie requested this!" She fetched it out and set it beside Tom, tracing her finger along the nearly indecipherable lines of old-fashioned curly script writing. "Aha! We have our answer. Right here!"

And Ella read aloud, "'*This tenancy agreement is duly set forth between the crown and parties, Millie Mercer and Sally Mercer.*' Right there in black and white! Millie has her answer. The agreement was between both the sisters."

Tomcat tapped a paw to the bottom of the old parchment deed. "But look here! Only Millie signed it! See."

Ella's eyes dropped to where he indicated. "Ohh, I see. Quite right. Hmm, that does throw a sandal in the works. Well, I can only pass on what we've found to Millie. Let's hope they can resolve their feud, and nothing will come of this revelation after all."

"They're fighting?" Tomcat asked. "But they always seem so in sync."

"Agreed." Ella placed the deed back on the pile and closed the drawer. "I rather think it might have started when Millie locked Sally out of the shop last month—do you remember? Accused her of being a werewolf because she ate Willow's brownies."

"Ohh! And that's when Olly, Sam, and Sandy helped Sally after she fainted on the steps! And now Sally is going to adopt Olly! So, some good did come out of it." Tomcat paced the length of the map drawers. "Hey! I've a thought! You should do a 'sweep' of the room for magic with Ace's rose spectacles!"

Ella felt around in her pocket and extracted the small frames. "That is a very good idea." She held the glasses up to her nose and squinted through them and then turned here and there to inspect the room. "I can't see anything...other than your glowing essence."

"Turn out the light!" Tomcat suggested. Jumping off the map drawers, he darted over to the comfy chair. "And I'll stay behind you, out of the way, so as not to interfere with the lighting."

Ella picked up the walking stick, flipped it over, and shut off the light. Once again, they were plunged into darkness. "Can't see my hand in front of my face," she muttered, doing just that—waving her hand in front of her. "I can't even see the drawer handles to open the wretched things... Oh, wait, I do see something..." She paused as something purple glowed faintly before her. Ella wiggled her fingers. "Ah, just a trick of the light. There must be some residual unicorn...er...magic, on my hands. Must have rubbed off from handling the dollar."

"You need to wash your hands better," Tomcat scolded.

"Thank you very much!" Ella replied, affronted that he might impugn her hygiene, before repeating the hunt through the map drawer with the aid of Ace's spectacles. A few minutes later, she stood and turned the walking stick light back on. "Nothing."

"Nothing!" Tomcat yowled. "There has to be! We've run out of clues! Cassidy is counting on us! Do it again. Look harder!" He leapt from the chair and hooked a paw about one of the map drawers, yanking it open with some effort.

Ella sighed and placed the little glasses away. "Tom, I know that Cassidy means a great deal to you, and loyalty is one of the qualities I admire in you. I feel as you, it's *unlikely* Cassidy was taking bribes, but—"

"Don't you dare say anything bad about Cass!" Tomcat hissed, his hackles running the length of his arched back. "She's not involved! She is *not* a crooked cop!"

"We just need to be sensible about this, be prepared for the worst, and then it won't hurt as much," Ella replied calmly.

"No!" Tomcat stomped on the flagstones. "She is innocent!" He pointed to the stout door. "Open this right now! You can give up if you want, but I am going to prove her innocence!"

Ella complied, opening the door for him. "Tom, be reasonable. We just need to consider all the possibilities."

"I *am* being reasonable! You're the one who is acting crazy!" And with that outburst, he fled down the corridor, a streak of indignant spikey white fur against the grey stones.

CHAPTER 27

THE BEST PEOPLE

BACK ROOMS, POST OFFICE, CHARMINGTON.

"Well done, Ella," Ella berated herself ironically as she trudged up the back staircase that led to the main post office level. "You could not have handled that better," she muttered.

Ella found herself 'behind the curtain' on the workers' side of the post office. It was a hive of industry back here. Clerks stationed in little cubicles sat at desks, bells dinging as they clacked away on typewriters. Other workers bustled here and there, moving trolleys full of parcels or sorting armfuls of letters into a giant wall of pigeonhole slots.

The walls were covered with posters, maps, colourful timetables, and schedules. Everything appeared modern and efficient. From the lemon-scented wood polish to the large clock on the wall positioned beside an oil painting of the queen. There was a second oil painting, only slightly less grand, of Harold Harper, too. Every element said that the Charmington post office was a well-oiled machine.

"Excuse me," Ella asked a chap in a red uniform with a little pillbox-style hat. She showed him the bundle of letters Willow had been mistakenly given for box number ninety-nine. "There's been a mix-up with the P.O. boxes."

He touched a hand to his hat in salute and pointed to the back of a woman in the far corner cubicle. "Hillary is in charge of the P.O. boxes."

Ella thanked him and walked on, breathing in deeply the lemon-scented wood polish that saturated the air. Goodness, every piece of woodwork was polished to a high sheen, and all the brass candlesticks shone brightly. Even with the vanity portrait of Harold hanging over the workers, inexplicably painted taller and thinner than in real life, surely this must be a nice place to work.

Hillary was at a desk, her back to Ella, a large stack of papers from an unwrapped parcel before her. She was quickly turning the pages over, one by one. "Hillary, my dear," Ella called out.

"Epp!" Hillary jumped, and the page in her hand fluttered to Ella's feet.

Ella picked it up and glanced at it on reflex. The words '*heaving bosom*' and '*run away tonight, my love! Escape the dastardly baron forever!*' jumped out at her.

"One of Tobias' stories, I take it?" Ella said with a chuckle and handed it over to Hillary, who had turned bright red.

"Oh, please tell me you won't report me!" She gestured to the unwrapped parcel.

Ella shrugged. "I expect Tobias would love to know he had a fan. If you like his stories, you should tell him. I think it would make his day."

Hillary puffed out a big breath of air across her fringe and laughed. "Oh, you're such a card, Good Mother Ella—but I *couldn't* tell him. I'm much too shy." She stood up, pushing the parcel behind her. "What can I help you with—oh! Do you want me to work for the tax office? Please say yes!"

Taken aback a little at Hillary's enthusiasm, Ella stuttered, "Well, no, er, I mean, I haven't had time to look over the staffing requirements." She showed Hillary the bundle of letters. "Willow collected these yesterday by accident. She hoped you'd be able to sort it?"

Hillary snatched the letters, her face an abject picture of horror. "Ugh! Yes, of course, this is entirely my fault, silly me. Actually, before you go, as I said before, there's a bit of mail for you too, in your P.O. box. Do you know where the private box room is?"

Ella was puzzled. "But I don't have a P.O. box…?"

Hillary tapped her arm with the bundle of letters, as if Ella were being modest. "Silly! It's a perk of the tax collector's job. As soon as Dad said the queen wanted you to take over, I started putting your mail in there. I knew you'd get the votes. It's through here. Shall I show you?"

Ella nodded. The girl seemed so eager to be helpful, and she was going to have to fathom this tax job sooner or later. Ella was led through to a private room somewhat resembling a stylish home office, located behind twin grand doors that were accessed from the public side of the foyer.

Inside, there were rows and rows of little brass doors lining the walls, all numbered with brass nameplates or neatly written parchment squares stating surnames. There was a plush seating area and a rather grand desk. "This is very nice," Ella said, feeling compelled to say something as Hillary pointed out the various amenities within the private box room, the magnifying glass on the desk, the free writing paper, and silver fountain pens.

"Oh yes, it's for our best people, naturally. You would *not* believe how many people are on the waiting list to rent a private box. They are quite coveted, I can tell you. Of course, we don't rent them to just *anyone*. There are standards."

Ella frowned. "But doesn't that mean you have to come *in* to collect your parcels and such? Rather than have them delivered to your door?"

Hillary chuckled, as if Ella was entirely missing the point. "But you also don't have your mail jostling in the postman's bag with all the *common* mail."

Ella just nodded, as that seemed the best response. "And which is my box?"

Hillary smacked her forehead as if appalled at this little oversight. "Of course. *How* could you know? The number is on your key attached to the chain of office. Didn't Goldilocks explain?"

"What key?" Ella asked, unlooping the gold chain from about her neck and inspecting the chunky ovals and little unicorn seal in case she had overlooked it before. There was no key.

Hillary blushed crimson again. "I am so sorry. Dad was meant to— I mean—*I'll take care of this* right away." She gently guided Ella over to the purple velvet chaise lounge, which seemed a touch elaborate and out of place in a post office. "Why don't you have a rest, just here, and I'll locate your box key as fast as I can. Help yourself to the complimentary sparkling mineral water or a cigar, and I will be back very soon!"

Dear, oh dear. Perhaps the post office wasn't quite the epitome of efficiency that Ella had assumed. Of course, everyone had their off days, even the best people...

Ella contemplated what Hillary had said before about the type of people apparently lined up to have their own private boxes.

"Hmm, the best people, and who exactly are they?" Ella perched on the chaise, her eyes drifting across the little brass P.O. box doors with the numbers and names. She saw the mayor's name, Sebastian. Did Sibylla have a box? Probably not. She definitely wouldn't see the value in spending time to come in to collect her mail when she could have it personally delivered.

Oh, there were Mercer and Mercer, the haberdashery twins. Their box was in the eighties. How exactly were the numbers chosen? By trying to match the box holder's physical street address? No, it must simply be a first-in, first-served sort of thing.

While she puzzled over this, Ella heard a strange noise. She cocked her head. What was it? Someone was sniffling... She leaned forward a bit to see if a child was hiding under the grand old desk. No...

"Tom," Ella said aloud to the otherwise empty room, "are you crying under the sofa?"

"Maybe," came back a familiar voice, followed by hiccups.

Ella's eyes drifted to P.O. number sixty-six. Willow's name had been placed on a neat little square of card over the original brass nameplate. Directly aligned under Willow's box was number ninety-nine. Ella was sympathising with how easy it would be to load mail into that box by mistake, when the brass nameplate on box ninety-nine made her rise out of her seat in alarm.

"Haversham!"

Chapter 28

Even the Best People Make Mistakes

Private Boxes Room, Post Office, Charmington.

"Haversham!" Ella repeated, clutching her hands to her cheeks. "Mrs. Haversham! It can't be...no, she's in Nottingham prison!" Ella strode over to the box doors in their neat rows lining the wall and stared at the nameplate.

Even up close, her eyes weren't deceiving her. Haversham was engraved on the brass nameplate of box ninety-nine.

Rooster's conversation from the morning drifted into Ella's mind. "No one escapes the Mrs...." Could he have been referring to *Mrs.* Haversham? "*Her* gang, he said *her* gang will kill him if he goes back to Nottingham prison. It can't be? Can it? Is Mrs. Haversham behind this whole thing?"

"Ella, what's wrong?" said Tomcat, peeping out from under the chaise lounge and wiping a paw across his tearful green eyes.

"Do you remember I told you my teacher, Mrs. Haversham, poisoned an apple in an attempt to get rid of me, but my sister Cinderella ate it by mistake?"

"Yes?" said Tom, his fluffy tail winding about the leg of the sofa.

"The poison was unicorn blood." Ella tapped the nameplate on the private box.

"A clue!" Tomcat jumped up on the desktop. "Quick! Open it! Use your Keys to the Kingdom gift!"

Ella blinked, but then rallied. "Watch the door for me!"

Tomcat leapt down from the desktop and pressed his furry face to the crack between the twin grand doors. "Clear!"

Heart in her throat, Ella yanked open the door of box number ninety-nine.

The private box was absolutely stuffed full of letters. Goodness, had these been accumulating for Mrs. Haversham over the decades the old witch had been in prison?

Ella grabbed a handful and spread them out on the desk. An odd collection presented itself before her. All were addressed to P.O. box ninety-nine, but not directly to Mrs. Haversham. Ella read some of the addresses aloud. "Holiday Fun in Sunny Nottingham competition... Nottingham Palace Job Application... Advice Column, *Nottingham Times*... What is all this? Is someone from Nottingham using the box?"

"Anything else in there?" Tomcat asked over his shoulder and then smooshed his face back to the door crack to watch for approaching people.

Ella pulled out another bundle of letters. Gosh, they were unexpectedly heavy. Had people posted coins? The movement of the letters nudged something tucked at the back. Ella reached into the mailbox, and her fingers brushed against something small, cylindrical, and ice cold.

"There's something in here..." she told Tom and grasped the freezing cold item, a crystal vial filled with purple-black liquid. Ella gulped. "Magic preserve..." *I think it's unicorn blood* was on her lips when the weighty object among the fistful of letters in her other hand revealed itself. A palm-sized metal rectangle slid from the pile and dropped onto her boot toe. "A printing plate!"

"Someone is coming!" Tomcat hissed, darting back from the door.

"The plate!" Ella cried, stuffing the vial in her pocket, and hurriedly cramming the letters back into box ninety-nine.

"I've got it!" Tomcat said, a streak of white fur, and he dived at her feet and up under her skirts as she slammed the little brass door shut.

Ella turned around slowly, trying to appear casual as Hillary and Harold burst into the room mid-argument.

"Can't even entrust Goldilocks with a simple task!" Harold was complaining to his daughter as Ella tried to school her face into a picture of serene innocence, while Tomcat, fumbling about under her skirt, was...? Ah. Was sliding the plate down the side of her boot.

"This is exactly why I can't promote you," Harold carried on, addressing his daughter as if Ella weren't even there. "I need you to fix up all the annoying, tedious, incompetent types."

"But, Dad, if I had more responsibility, I could still do all those things," Hillary responded. "And maintain the ledgers."

When Hillary said the word *ledgers,* she gave Ella a sharp, knowing look, as if she were trying to communicate something. Was she trying to prove to Ella her capabilities with numbers? Hillary had said something about her father not being able to refuse should Ella personally request Hillary join the tax team, and the indications were the young woman didn't enjoy working at the post office.

Ella cleared her throat. "Ledgers, you say? Are you good with accountancy? I'm sure the tax department would welcome—"

"Hillary misspoke," Harold interrupted Ella, cutting her off. "Hillary meant rosters, didn't you? I'm the only one who touches the ledgers."

"Yes, Dad," Hillary said, tight-lipped, eyes downcast, as Harold extracted the key on the length of chain from his waistcoat pocket and set it to the lock on P.O. box number five.

Goodness, did his key open *all* the private boxes as well as *all* the building's doors? It truly must be a master key. No wonder Harold was so grumpy at Hillary for losing not one but two of those keys, assuming hers were also masters—it was no small security matter, after all.

Harold stood aside, gesturing to the unlocked box door. "Madame."

Ella opened the little door. As Hillary forewarned, there was a large parcel and several letters within. Oh dear, that parcel would be cumbersome to carry. Perhaps she could dump it up in her tax collector's office until she had time to investigate it later?

Hillary must have seen Ella's sour expression because she said, "Allow me. The parcel is quite heavy." Ella nodded, and Hillary emptied the contents of the private mailbox and piled it up onto the desk for Ella.

The parcel was from Merlin, and it was suspiciously commemorative *Guide*-sized. There were also a few letters for Tom from Master Spicer, his friend at the Nottingham orphanage where Tom had grown up. To top it off, there was a rather elaborate golden envelope with the royal crest of the Regent of Nottingham, Prince John. "Whatever can this be?" Ella said, looking at the shiny letter.

"That's an invite to the coronation!" Hillary said enviously, nudging the thick golden envelope. "The mayor got one too!"

"Is there anything *else* we can *assist* you with today?" Harold said tightly, talking over Hillary as if somehow the missing private box key was all Ella's fault, and he was being terribly inconvenienced by the whole affair.

Behind his back, Hillary mouthed, "Dad didn't get an invite."

Suppressing a smirk, Ella imagined Harold consoling this social snub in his blueprint room later on tonight while having a bit of a sulk, drinking whiskey and eating chocolates, surrounded by dusty old newspapers and ledgers.

Ledgers! Ella suppressed a gasp. A jolt of comprehension popped into her mind. Hillary had been trying to inform her of something about ledgers! *Magic preserve.* Was Harold *hiding* some dodgy accounting within those neat little rows of columns and figures?

Follow the money, Rooster had said, *follow the money!*

A cunning plan suddenly presented itself in Ella's mind, and she asked, "Speaking of assistance, you know, with all the drama this morning, I completely forgot the task I was trying to complete regarding the tenancy deeds stored in your blueprint room. I can't remember the way. All the underground corridors look the same. Would one of you show me?"

Tomcat moved under Ella's skirts from where he had now clamped himself about her boot, and he tapped the back of her knees as if to say, *but we did that already*. Ella focused on not reacting while Tomcat's whiskers tickled her skin.

"I am more than happy to show you the way," Hillary volunteered, her smile wide as if things were finally going her way. "But I'd need your key, Dad." She held out her hand.

Harold's face fell. He brushed his palm against the straining buttons on his silk vest. "Ah, yes, that reminds me. Axel found your key, Hillary. He dropped it back, just before. I put it on your desk. Didn't you see?"

"I'm sure it wasn't there a moment ago." Hillary frowned.

"While Hillary hunts for her key, you could show me to the blueprint room, Harold," Ella pressed. Whenever Sibylla felt a servant was being a bit difficult, she gave them plenty of meaningless tasks to remind them of their place, but Ella had quite another plan in mind...

"Well, I am rather busy, and Hillary is more suited to the task. Just wait here. She'll be back in a moment. Hillary, if you could assist Madame Charming, and now if you'll excuse me..."

Ella stepped in front of both of them to block their exit. "You know what, never mind. Tomorrow will do just as well for me to *rummage* around in the blueprint room. It's not an urgent task. If you'll just give me the room, I'll attend to my *private* correspondence..." She picked up the golden envelope and waited expectantly.

Harold smoothed his waistcoat again and snapped at Hillary, "Well, child, don't leave the key unattended on your desk..." And he departed from the private room with Hillary glumly trailing after him.

Ella hooked up her skirt and whispered down to Tomcat, who was clamped like a baby monkey on her boot, "Quick, make use of your cat disguise, and go stake out the blueprint room..."

"But..." protested Tom.

"Trust me. Meet me in the tax office later."

CHAPTER 29

SNITCHES GET YELLOW BRITCHES

TAX OFFICE, ATTIC OF THE TOWN HALL, CHARMINGTON.

Anyone witnessing Ella limp her way up the staircase of the town hall would have noticed nothing out of the ordinary. Ella was well known for her arthritic knees. They weren't to know that today's limp was entirely down to the printing plate awkwardly stashed in her right boot.

Burdened by the parcel from Merlin, letters for Tom, and the invitation from Prince John, Ella fumbled with the door handle to her tax office.

The attic office was far more appealing than Ella had been expecting. The main room was large, and there were various desks, tables, and many windows overlooking Northgate Square far below. The whole office was pleasantly warm due to a series of radiators lining the room.

Robinne was asleep at one, her boots up on the radiator, while she rocked back on an office chair.

Ella thumped the heavy parcel onto a nearby desk, and Robinne tumbled from her sleep, alert and ready to run. "Oh, it's just you," she said, on seeing Ella, and let out a sigh of relief.

"Axel didn't catch you, then?" Ella said, stating the obvious as Robinne joined her at the desk.

Robinne crossed her arms and wrapped her scarlet cloak about herself, recalling the early morning chase. "I *didn't* take the Mossfern whiskey, and it's really rich of Axel claiming the whiskey, which Arthur paid for, is even his to claim."

"Mossfern whiskey, you say? Are you sure?" Ella untied the string from Merlin's parcel and then ripped off the paper. She groaned.

A fancy commemorative edition of *The Guide* was within, so fancy it had a little golden clasp lock. She picked up a note on top of the book.

Dear Miss Charming, thank you for your recent enquiry about scholarships to Camelot Academy of Magic—Avalon's premier magical institution. Unfortunately, we cannot accommodate your request at this time. Please find enclosed a luxury, special edition of The Guide, *with our compliments.*

"A form letter! Not even written by Merlin. He really is the pits," Ella moaned, sliding the elaborate *Guide* over to Robinne. "Do you think we can sell this? Is it worth anything?"

"The illustrated editions are always quite collectable, especially the ones with the misprint where the magpie pictures were swapped for penguins." Robinne tapped the little brass lock clasping the large volume shut. "Did he include the key? We can probably force it, but that would reduce the value."

"Merlin, you old fool!" Ella grumbled, touching the clasp. The lock gave way. She opened the book and stepped back, surprised by what she saw. The book had been hollowed out.

Inside were several thin journals of some kind. Robinne picked one up and read the title aloud, "*Basic Magic for Beginners*! Oh, this is a *textbook*." She pointed to the authorial credit. "Written by Merlin. These are *so* illegal, and people call *me* a rebel when Ella, you're the one harbouring contraband!"

"Merlin, you cunning old goat," Ella muttered to herself. So, her brother had come through after all. And now, armed with the knowledge hidden in these beginner textbooks, hopefully the Chelton's son, Cheapcuts, could self-teach the basics of magic. Her thoughts drifted back to the orphan siblings, Sandy and Sam, who were also displaying magical abilities. If these books proved useful, she would have to request more copies. "Speaking of contraband..." She extracted the printing plate from out of her boot.

Robinne blinked. "How did that get in there?"

"Do not ask," Ella quipped, and she set the plate down to decipher the backwards text.

Robinne tilted her head. "Um, what is this? It's got 'hundred' written backwards?"

Ella hummed. Well, well, well. "This, my dear, is the missing piece."

"Really? Because it looks like it's *missing* something. Why would you just print the word *hundred*? It doesn't make any sense."

"This simple device can overprint money, paper money, turning 'one' into 'one hundred', and it will make you rich beyond your wildest dreams..." Ella said, feeling in her pocket for the icy vial. "Provided you have the secret hallucinogenic ingredient to convince the brain that what you're seeing is real." She also fetched Ace's glasses and cautiously held them over the vial, but not close to her eyes. A flare of intense crimson lit up her hand, and Robinne jumped back. "What is that? Is that magic?"

Ella nodded grimly. "Black magic. The final nail in the coffin, I'm afraid."

But for who?

Ella placed the vial and glasses back in separate pockets. "I don't suppose you heard a certain argument last night? Between Cassidy and Ace, outside the post office? Marge said you were with her."

"I wasn't *with her*. Marge was telling me off again for wearing my red cloak." Robinne flicked through one of the magic textbooks. "But yeah, I heard the argument. It was a bit odd. So what if Cass wanted to attend Axel's party? Free drinks on offer is a good bribe. I'm not surprised she overlooked her dislike of Axel for that. I would have, too, but it would hurt my reputation."

"Bribes?" Ella listened up intently. "What do you mean?"

"Yeah, Ace said it wasn't worth her pride. Such bribes were not worth the cost."

"So, you *don't* think they were arguing about money? Money bribes?"

Robinne looked puzzled, as if recalling what she'd heard. "I guess it *could* have been money. I just assumed it was about the free drinks, that the drinks were bribes. Why else would she want to go? Cassidy and Axel don't exactly get along. Like I said, it was odd. Cass isn't the sort to stand around airing her dirty laundry. And Ace kept grinning as he shouted. It was like watching a play."

"Free drinks, free drinks," Ella muttered. "It all seems to lead back to drink. Rooster should have said 'follow the alcohol', rather than 'follow the money.'"

Robinne flicked back and forth through some of the textbook pages, a slightly concerned expression on her heart-shaped face. "Actually...now you mention it, and I didn't want to say this when Tom was around, but Wulf and I were at the Huntsman last week, and Cass joined us. She was asking Wulf a lot of questions about what it was like working for Prince John. About the pay rates, the cost of stuff in Nottingham. I kind of think she's considering moving there..."

"Oh dear," Ella muttered, thinking this information over. "Tom will not like that news."

"Exactly," Robinne agreed, "I didn't want him to find that out from me..." She suddenly ducked under the desk, and Ella turned to the office door as two shadows, one tall and one short, were cast over the wavy glass, followed by a tentative knock.

"Come in, it's open," Ella called, quickly placing the printing plate into a desk drawer, and shutting *The Guide* closed, with its stash of banned textbooks once more securely locked within.

Sally peeked around the door. She was wearing a tall yellow bonnet festooned with white ostrich feathers, and holding the hand of a very tearful Olly, likewise dressed in bold yellow, but with noticeably less lace than this morning.

Oh dear, had Olly found out about the tea and cake invitation to Sam and Sandy and felt left out? Well, that was easily remedied.

"Olly has something they would like to say, don't you, dear?" said Sally, with a gentle and patient tone. "Go on, dear, you'll feel better. Tell Her Highness what you told me."

Olly shook their head, tears and snot streaming down their reddened face. They gulped, a tearful shudder, and said, "Ain't a snitch!"

Ella went to Olly's side and guided the pair to a circle of striped wingback chairs beside a big radiator and a very dead potted plant. "Whatever is the matter, my dear? You can tell me." She crossed her fingers and touched her earlobes. "Double Cat Lady promise, you will not be in trouble."

"I...I turned out all the streetlamps so people would trip and drop stuff!" Olly managed in a breathy confession. "But that ain't the worst!" They wiped a yellow velvet-covered arm across their face and then burst out in a waterfall of tears, "I snitched, and I got Miss Cassidy hurt, didn't I? It's all my fault! I told Ace's message to Axel!"

CHAPTER 30

NOT QUITE THE FINAL PIECE

TAX OFFICE, ATTIC OF THE TOWN HALL, CHARMINGTON.

"I'm so—so—sorry," Olly stammered, wiping their tears and snot across the lovely yellow outfit that no doubt Sally had spent many hours fashioning. But Sally just tenderly patted the child's hand, and Ella had a warm feeling that young Olly had found a loving home in which they would thrive.

Ella felt in her pocket and extracted the handkerchief that Doctor Hyde had given her that day. She passed it to the elderly haberdashery owner, who nodded her thanks and passed it over to the distressed child.

Ella sat on the blue-striped chair opposite Olly. "Your remorse does you credit, child. You know you have acted poorly, but I give you my word that Miss Cassidy will heal and be fine. And when she does get better, I hope you will have the courage to apologise to Cassidy in person, and if you do, I will come with you and lend you my support."

"And I," Sally added, covertly wiping away a tear of her own.

Olly snuffled a bit more and scrubbed their face with the silk handkerchief. "You promise she's going to be okay?"

Ella nodded solemnly. "I give you my word as the cat lady."

Olly glanced up at their ostrich feather-bedecked caregiver. "Missus Sally says you're a real princess, even though you're very old?"

"That too," Ella added as Sally blushed. "And the oath of a princess cat lady is the strongest oath there is. Yes?" As Olly's tears had dried up, Ella took the opportunity to say, "Now, why don't you tell me what else happened last night when you went to the sheriff's party?"

Olly cast one glance up at Sally, as if for permission, who nodded, and then they began recounting their story. "I only went there 'cos Mr. Ace asked me."

"Yes, I remember. Mr. Ace had asked you to go find Cassidy to give her an important message that he had seen Rooster in the cluckoo shop basement."

Sally suddenly paled and clutched her yellow pelisse jacket to her throat. "The criminal Rooster! I've seen his wanted posters! Child, you should have come to me! Rooster is a dangerous man!"

Ella placed a hand on Sally's knee. "Next time, I'm sure Olly will do just that. Won't you, Olly?"

Olly made a shrugging motion that didn't imply agreement one way or the other. "But I couldn't find Miss Cassidy right away. And Mr. Axel caught me, and he made me, he *made* me tell him Ace's message. And when I did, he said that there was a fat bounty on Rooster's head, and he was going to collect it before Cassidy. And he shut me in the pantry, and no one found me for ages."

Hmm, so Axel had intercepted the message from Ace... Ella thought over this new piece of information. "How long between when you spoke to Axel and then Cassidy, do you know?"

"Ages." The child counted on their fingers. "Two pots of jam, some honey and bread, half a turnip—I thought it was an apple. It was very dark in the pantry. Couldn't see what I was eating."

"Too dark... Couldn't see..." Ella repeated. Something about the child's description was making her sixth-sense prickle. But why? "What about the town hall cluckoo clock? Did you hear it striking?"

"Were too noisy in the cupboard. There were lots of voices and music playing outside."

Ella stood up and paced in front of the dead potted plant. "I see..." All that really mattered was it was clear that Axel had a head start on Cassidy. And somehow Rooster ended up locked in the new cells under the police station, and Axel would be able to claim his bounty. So why fabricate the story that Rooster had been captured *two* days beforehand?

"Thank you, Olly, you've been very helpful," Ella said, holding out her hand for Olly to shake, which they did, and then they made a bow followed by a curtsey.

"Olly hasn't decided which style they prefer yet," Sally added, as if feeling the need to justify the unusual salutation, as Ella walked the pair to the door. "Thank you so much for your time today, Your Highness. I know you're very busy."

Ella swallowed. No doubt she was going to be stuck with Sally addressing her as *highness* from now on. But it was a small price to pay, and oddly enough, it did seem to make the woman happy. "I hope

I am never too busy for the concerns of Charmington's citizens," Ella said honestly.

"And congratulations on the new job," Sally offered, stopping in the doorway. "Are you going to have a little soirée? Celebration drinks, perhaps?"

Ella had been about to say a firm *no* when a thought occurred. "Actually, Hillary suggested something similar, and while the idea didn't immediately strike me, I was just thinking it would be convenient to round up a few people and speak to everyone at the same time...

"And, as I have already invited Olly's friends, Sam and Sandy, to supper here tonight, I might as well extend the invitation and have a little get-together to mark the occasion of this new job. I would be honoured if you, Millie, and Olly would join me. I have ordered pies from Betty, and I expect Willow can be counted on to provide cakes and brownies afterwards..."

"That sounds delightful," Sally enthused. "Olly and I will pop around earlier and bring some bunting to decorate the office!"

When Ella closed the door a moment later, she turned back into the room to see Robinne bowing low. "All hail, Princess Cat Lady!"

"Very funny," Ella muttered. "If you're not careful, I might start bestowing titles of my own. Would you prefer Princess Unicorn or Pretty-Pretty Prancing Pony..." Ella's half-hearted threats drifted off as she heard another knock on the office door. Goodness, it was constantly go, go, go up here.

But it was only Tomcat at the door. He rushed into the office and jumped up on the desktop and sat beside the hollowed-out commemorative copy of *The Guide.*

"Well, which one did you catch going back to the blueprint room?" Ella interjected before he could talk. "Hillary or Harold?"

"Wait! You *knew* that would happen?" Tomcat enquired, tilting his little cat head to one side.

"Can one of you please explain what's going on?" Robinne interrupted. "I'm feeling left out."

And so Tomcat and Ella explained the day's events, ending in Ella saying, "And it occurred to me that whoever had something to hide, if they knew I was going to go back to the blueprint room to have a *proper* look around, even if they had already moved whatever they were trying to hide, they would go back and make sure there wasn't anything else to implicate them. It's human nature. So, who was it, Tom? Hillary or Harold?"

"Ha!" Tomcat said, his whiskers fanning. "You forgot one possibility—it was both of them!"

"Both?" Ella blinked and crossed her arms. "Go on, then, tell us what you heard and saw."

"Harold was very cross at Hillary. He kept saying things like she'd never get a promotion, and he was a clerk who worked his way to the top, and she had to do the same thing, and there'd be no shortcuts." Tomcat took a breath. "And then they moved all the ledgers that were piled on the blueprint drawers and carried them upstairs to Harold's office, and he locked them in his desk." Tomcat sat back and crossed his arms over his fluffy tummy. "What do you make of that?"

"That is very interesting," Ella murmured, thinking over what Tom had reported. "And well done you, you have definitely proved the worth of your cat disguise today."

"What do you think Harold is up to?" Robinne asked. "Embezzlement?"

"Possibly. We'll have to find someone very good at numbers and have them look through those account books, that's for sure..."

"You could ask Hansel,," Robinne suggested. "I nearly tripped over him last week because he was lying in the middle of West Avenue counting cobblestones to figure out what was the average number of cobbles per square foot across the entire town."

"Really?" Ella's hopes perked up. "That definitely sounds like the kind of candidate we should have on the tax team. I don't suppose I can also convince either of you to join?"

"Do I get an office and Monday to Friday off?" Robinne asked while Tom's attention was drawn to the fancy copy of *The Guide*.

He flipped the large volume open, then stared wide-mouthed at the hollowed-out middle filled with magical textbooks. "Look! Ella, Look!"

Oh dear...Had she not relocked the book's clasp? That was careless. "Yes, thank you, we know," Ella replied distractedly, as she thought back over her conversation with young Olly and Sally. There was something about Olly's pantry comment that was tugging at her mind, something she couldn't quite fathom. *I couldn't see what I was eating...*

Tomcat shut *The Guide* and stared. "When it's closed, it just looks like an ordinary book! No one would ever know what's hidden in the pages."

Ella did a double-take. "Say that again?"

Tomcat shrugged. "I just said no one would ever suspect something was hidden between the pages."

"Hidden in the pages…" Ella repeated to herself in wonderment, and she spread *The Guide* open and watched the cut pages fan out around the hidden contraband. "Quite so! Tom, this is an excellent clue! In fact, I think this is the final clue!"

"It is…?" Tomcat pulled a face.

Ella clapped her hands. "Right, we need to get everything in order and gather all the necessary people here for my big announcement." She pointed at Tomcat. "Tom, will you please go fetch Dirk and the new doctor, and request that Willow bring a tray or two of her brownies, plus make sure Willow brings Tobias—I need another word with him."

Tomcat's ears flattened. "Ella, this is no time for a party!"

"I agree with you, Tom. As Nigella Pickford would say, it's time for the Third Act when the villains are uncovered! Now, when you send Dirk here, you stay at the hospital and watch over Cassidy with Gretel. As for me, I shall go fetch Goldilocks, plus others from the council. And everyone should meet back here at precisely seven o'clock."

Robinne leaned on the desktop. "What can I do?"

Ella smiled broadly. "You, my dear, have the most important job. You shall be in charge of fetching the drinks. I have an idea where a particularly fine vintage is hiding…"

CHAPTER 31

ELLA'S TAX OFFICE PARTY

TAX OFFICE, ATTIC OF THE TOWN HALL, CHARMINGTON.

After tracking down the members of the council that Ella had met with only that morning and personally delivering her invitation to come up to the attic tax office for a little informal party, Ella turned her attention to her prior engagement, the six-thirty supper with the Baker Street orphans, Sam and Sandy.

Sally, Olly, and Millie arrived with armfuls of bunting and fairy lights. "The fairy lights don't work anymore," Sally apologised, "but they're all stitched in with the cloth bunting."

"No need to apologise," Ella said. "They still look pretty, like little spring blooms." And together they decorated the tax office with the colourful streamers.

Just before six-thirty, Betty herself arrived with a large selection of dainty miniature pies encased in golden pastry. Betty, whom Ella had known as a child, was now well into her seventies. She had a shy little great-granddaughter in tow, who kept one hand on her grandmama's apron string at all times and couldn't be coaxed into saying a word, even by the chatty Olly, who talked non-stop and pointed out all the interesting objects within the office, like the typewriters, the dead potted plant, and the radiators, as if they were giving a tour of a grand home.

As the cluckoo clock in the tower somewhere above the attic office crowed the half-hour, Sam and Sandy arrived with Mr. Rat perched on Sam's shoulder and wearing a little top hat fashioned from a scrap of felt.

On spying Mr. Rat, Betty sighed, but her little granddaughter giggled, and suddenly the lifeless fairy lights sputtered and sparkled and then glowed steadily, filling the room with pretty colours, pink, blue, and green.

"Oh!" Millie clutched her hand to her mouth, and tears sprang to her eyes. "These lights haven't worked for decades! You made them for my engagement party..." she said to Sally, and whatever private argument the pair were having seemed to find a moment of truce as Sally went to her side and patted her shoulder in a consoling manner.

"Oh, it's so beautiful…" murmured Sandy, staring up at the colourful strings looped across the window frames while Sam held Mr. Rat up for a closer look.

"It's like being inside a rainbow," Olly added in awe.

Ella cast a glance at Betty, who, unlike everyone else, wore a tight expression, and she stood as if to shield her little granddaughter from the adults. "Beg pardon, Mistress," Betty said to Ella, "she can't help herself. T'aint her fault. She don't mean no harm."

Ella cast her gaze across the collection of children. So, it would appear that more than just Sam and Sandy had some innate Wyld magical ability. She glanced at the desk in which she had tucked away Merlin's copy of *The Guide*. One set of Merlin's beginners' textbooks wasn't going to be enough…

Ella smiled warmly at Betty and the little girl hiding behind her. "I love fairy lights. I am always happy to see them glowing. They bring joy to my heart."

"Hear, hear," Sally piped up.

"And I most of all," Millie added, with a sudden sharp look at her sister, as if whatever they had been fighting about had reignited her competitive streak.

Everyone sat down to supper, and Ella negotiated with Betty to allow Mr. Rat within Betty's pie shop provided Sam adhered to a strict set of guidelines, which mostly involved Sam keeping Mr. Rat on their person at all times and not letting any other customers see him.

Soon after that, Betty excused herself and her granddaughter, and Ella prepared for the next round of guests. Millie offered to provide some wine glasses from their home, and, along with Sally and Sandy, they went to fetch them, while Olly and Sam volunteered to stay and take people's coats as they slowly filtered in.

"Welcome, welcome," Ella said as Axel arrived, and he gave Ella a very narrowed-eyed look, suspicious at the warmth in her greeting, but nonetheless he found himself a perch on one of the radiators and even took a pastry when Sam offered the tray.

"May I take your coat, sir?" Olly said, bowing before Harold, the postmaster, and his daughter, as they peered around the glass door.

"No, you may not!" Harold snapped, and he unbuttoned his coat and dumped it on Hillary's arm before she even had time to remove her own. "Didn't I ban you from the post office for picking pockets?"

"I fink you must have confused me with some street urchin," Olly answered, gesturing to their fine yellow velvet outfit. "Clearly, I am a toff."

Confident that Olly wouldn't be intimidated by Harold's gruff bullying, Ella went to assist the haberdashery twins and Sandy as they arrived with the empty wine glasses, but Tobias had met them on the stairs and was already offering his assistance.

Willow arrived next, bringing a tray of her famous brownies, which were eagerly welcomed, and she was shortly followed by the doctor in his long black duster coat, along with Dirk.

Dirk looked terrible, pale and twitchy. Oh dear, did he still have those potentially black magic-stained one-hundred-dollar notes tucked into his tricorn?

"Not sure I should leave Cass," Dirk muttered to Ella, and she patted his shoulder.

"With Tom and Gretel watching over her, I'm sure she is in safe hands," Ella began, but just then Goldilocks arrived, and the little lady's usually bright and sunny expression fell on seeing Dirk.

"What's he doing here?" Goldi huffed. "I wouldn't have come if I'd known he was going to be here, after what his niece did to my friend."

"Trust me, please, all will be revealed shortly," Ella said, which earned another huff of displeasure, but Goldilocks stomped into the office and found herself a spot as far away from Dirk as she could manage, muttering things about Cassidy under her breath.

And then Ella whispered to Willow, "Can you please keep an eye on Dirk and make sure his tricorn stays off? He has some of those tainted banknotes tucked in there, and I think he's suffering the side effects of magical delusions..."

Ella looked about the room. Everyone was there except for Robinne. She took the time to make introductions and encourage small talk. "Doctor Hyde, this is Tobias. He's also a writer. Doctor Hyde has a book published on poisons." The gentlemen shook hands, but before either could speak, Sally turned to the doctor.

"You have a book out?" she enquired. "I hold a popular book club. We're always looking for new books to discuss."

"*We* have a book club," Millie corrected peevishly. "It was entirely my idea, after all."

Ella turned away as the twins began bickering. Dear, oh dear, whatever had come between them? She went to assist Hillary and the children, who were hanging up the last of the coats.

Just then, Robinne arrived, and judging from her grin, she had found the alcohol that Ella had sent her to find. Ella closed the office door now that everyone was here. She motioned to young Sandy. "Would you mind playing guard duty and call my name if anyone attempts to leave?" Sandy snapped off a sharp salute, and Sam and Olly, sensing some game was afoot, likewise stood in front of the door.

Robinne carried the cardboard box balanced on her hip to the central table that Ella gestured to, where they had the empty wine glasses waiting. She lifted a bottle of Mossfern whiskey from out of the box and arched an eyebrow at Ella.

"Hey!" Axel uttered, suddenly recognising the whiskey. He stood up from his sulky slouch against the radiator and strode over to the table in the middle of the room. "That's *my* whiskey! I *knew* you stole it!"

"I did not," Robinne replied, hands on hips.

All the small talk ceased, and Ella clapped her hands to focus everyone's attention on her. "Ladies and gentlemen, thank you so much for attending my little gathering. Now that the drinks have arrived, we can begin with the true reason I have asked you all here tonight." This announcement drew some confused looks and some murmurings, which Ella ignored, stating, "Sheriff, would you please do the honours and fill the glasses?"

"About time!" Axel agreed, and he thumbed out the cork of one bottle and filled the nearest glass. A deep emerald-green liquid flowed into the clear crystal. "What the—?" Axel exclaimed, and everyone crowded closer, muttering similar exclamations of confusion. Axel tipped the whiskey bottle and cautiously sniffed the neck opening. "What is this? Is this ink? Yuck. What trick are you playing, old woman?"

His rude comment drew horrified gasps from the haberdashery twins, but Ella, undeterred, said to Robinne, "Where did you find the bottles, my dear?"

"Exactly where you suspected they'd be," Robinne replied. "At Hillary's flat."

Everyone's gaze now swung to Hillary.

"Care to explain," Ella said to the post office clerk, "or shall I do it for you?"

Hillary baulked, and she backed up a step, her gaze glancing to the doorway where the three little orphans were all marching back and forth to stop anyone trying to leave. "I have no idea what you're implying. It's not a crime to put ink in a whiskey bottle."

"It's *more* than a little unconventional, though," began Millie, rather loudly, to a curt, "Shush, sister! I want to hear the next part," from Sally.

Ella replied with a sigh, "A fair point. Ink is just ink, unless, of course, it's Pendragon Green, which many of you won't have heard of. But Pendragon Green is a special ink used only in the creation of Avalon's paper currency."

Harold huffed out a breath. "How can you prove that claim? Regardless, I fail to see what this has to do with my daughter."

Ella conceded the point. "Quite so. Rather unfortunately, our forensic expert was killed last night, right after he discovered a secret printing press and a bunch of Avalon banknotes with their values altered."

Gasps spilt from the gathered guests.

"And the thing with this particular batch of counterfeits is someone had been mixing another key ingredient." Ella held the tatty and stained one dollar aloft and then put it on the table and stood back. "This black splotch is unicorn blood. A black magic ingredient that causes hallucinations. So, first the blood is bespelled to induce a gold fever or some other charm of desire, and then, when mixed into the Pendragon Green, it can make low-value one-dollar banknotes *feel* as high-value one-hundred-dollar banknotes. Completely undetectable fakes."

This bold claim drew several chuckles. "Would someone please care to demonstrate?" Ella said. "But just hold it for a moment. I must warn you, its effects are unhealthy for exposed periods of time."

Willow bumped into Dirk and knocked his hat off. The coachman gulped and picked up his tricorn and held it in trembling hands.

"I'll not be fooled," Millie scoffed. "Even with my eyesight, that's clearly only one dollar." But when she held the money, the haberdashery twin immediately changed her tune. "Just like you said, this is really valuable money. I know it in my bones."

"Don't be ridiculous. Whatever are you playing at, Sister? This blotch wouldn't fool a child." Sally snatched the money from her sibling's hand and held it aloft. "See! I am confident this is a *real* banknote—worth at least a year's wages."

Millie just tutted. "Who's the fool now?"

"What's going on?" Tobias asked as the note was handed around.

"This is the effect of black magic," Willow explained. "Anyone who touches the note is under its spell."

"I have no idea what your point is, but regardless of the *supposed* value, it's still worthless," Harold interjected sourly. "Even at the post office, we don't accept Avalon currency. No one in Charmington could spend it, no matter how much or how little it is worth."

Ella rolled her eyes. Trust Harold to be tiresome and forever trying to undermine her. She'd be lying if she said she wasn't looking forward to this... "Can anyone explain what Harold *fails* to comprehend?"

The others looked at each other somewhat blankly, and Ella was about to speak up when, fortunately, a youthful voice said gleefully, "You don't spend it!" piped up one of the Baker Street orphans from down at Sally's elbow.

"That's right," added Olly, wiping their nose as they climbed up onto a chair to better address the adults crowding around. "You don't spend it, you takes it down to the big city, and you swaps it for *proper* money!"

Sandy turned to their sibling, Sam, and said in a loud pantomime voice, "Hello, Nottingham money-lender person, I am a weary traveller from a far distant land. What is the current exchange rate for this high-value banknote, which ain't fake?"

Sam mimed handing back something heavy. "Please have this big bag of gold."

"Ahh, from the mouths of babes," Ella added with a smile at the dawning gasps of comprehension around her.

Axel whistled in admiration. "Worthless paper for gold. That is a scam!" He cast a shrewd glance at Ella, as if she had gone up somewhat in his esteem. "But unicorn blood is rarer than gold. Much rarer. How can you be sure it was being used?"

Ella's fingers brushed against the cold glass vial she had found and was now stowed in her skirt pocket. "A stash was kept in a defunct P.O. box."

"What?" The elderly haberdashery twins clutched each other in fright and looked around, staring at their neighbours. "Whose private box?"

"Mrs. Haversham's. Who, as some of you will be aware, has been in prison for going on twenty years, so clearly, she hasn't been using the P.O. box for quite some time..." Ella glanced up to see that Hillary was creeping for the door, but Robinne had moved to intercept her. "Hillary, aren't you in charge of the master key to the P.O. boxes?"

More gasps spilt from the older ladies' wrinkled throats and lace hankies were pressed to drooping bosoms in morbid fascination as the young post office woman stuttered, "I—I lost my key last night. You know I did! You *all* know I did!"

"Aha! Axel found it!" Harold cried, pointing at the new sheriff. "You returned it to me yourself this afternoon. You can't deny that. There were witnesses!"

"Ahh! Just so!" Millie cried, pointing a finger at Axel. "And last night, you were in the alley! I loaned you a lantern!"

"That doesn't prove anything, you old bag," Axel grumbled, oblivious to the chorus of shocked mumblings from horrified guests, while he opened up all the remaining bottles of Mossfern in desperation that his beloved whiskey might still be contained in one.

"No, possession of the key doesn't prove anything," Ella spoke into the appalled silence. "But I rather think this might." From her other skirt pocket, she withdrew Ace's broken rose-coloured glasses. "These belonged to Ace. I have a feeling this is what alerted him to the presence of unicorn blood. Black magic leaves a distinct residue, you see. Even when washed off, the magical glow remains for some time... Goldilocks, would you do the honours and check Hillary's hands?"

"My hands!" cried Hillary in abject horror. "Why do you want to check *my* hands? Surely, you mean Axel's hands."

"An excellent question, my dear. And if you will care to indulge me, I have a question of my own for you. How did you know?"

"How did I know what?" Hillary said, looking left and right as all eyes were on her.

Ella walked around Hillary to put herself between Hillary and the door. "This morning. How did you know that Ace and Cassidy were in the blueprint room?"

"Well, I saw them," Hillary mumbled.

Ella held up a finger. "Ah, but you didn't. You were in that room but a second or two when you shouted, 'Help! Help! Ace and Cassidy are dead.' But here's the thing. As soon as that door is closed, the room is pitch black. I've tested it myself. You can't see a thing. So, you didn't 'see' them. You *knew* they were there because you dumped them there."

CHAPTER 32

THE PIECES FALL INTO PLACE

EVERYONE STANDING CLOSE TO HILLARY suddenly took a horrified step backwards.

"Goldi, if you please. Check Hillary's hands for magical residue." Ella held out the broken pair of glasses to Goldilocks, but another person stepped forward.

"Ahem. There is no need," Harold interrupted, approaching Axel with his hands aloft. "I confess. I did it. I am the perpetrator." He held out his wrists to Axel as if to be shackled. "Take me away, sir."

Ella placed the rose-coloured glasses in Goldilocks' outstretched palm. "Your gallantry is duly noted, Harold. Perhaps you will provide everyone here with a full confession and recount how exactly you killed Ace?"

Harold blustered, coughed, and dropped eye contact. "Er, well, naturally, I bludgeoned him with the, er, brass candlestick."

Ella caught the eye of the tall, thin man wrapped in a floor-length black coat, who was standing at the back of the room and cautiously sniffing a brownie. "Doctor?"

The room fell silent as everyone turned to face the pale newcomer.

"Ahem. The craftsman called Ace was poisoned." The doctor slipped the brownie back onto the tray and wiped his fingers on his coat. "Unicorn blood is very toxic to the magical races."

Ella nodded. "Hillary, please hold out your hands. This will just take a moment." She motioned to Goldilocks to go ahead.

Hillary's face distorted in protest, but Dirk placed a hand on her shoulder. "If you are innocent, then you have nothing to fear."

"Fine!" Hillary growled, shaking off his touch. "But you're making a mistake."

Goldilocks held the bent and damaged little pink lens to one eye and squinted through the tinted glass.

The room held its collective breath.

"Ohh, goodness, her hands do glow purple!" the tiny woman exclaimed and then swept the lens over the rapt crowd. "Ohh, so do Axel's—and Dirks! Wait, and mine too!"

Harold snorted at Ella. "You foolish old woman. A *glow* thing doesn't prove anything except that we all touched this banknote!" He snatched up the stained one-dollar note from the office desk. "And this banknote is quite real. It's certainly real and valuable money. So, I don't know what the fuss is about."

There was a general sigh as Ella, deflated, raised her finger. "Ah yes, handing around the magical banknote to everyone present. I didn't think that through, did I?"

"I like a joke as much as the next person," Hillary snapped, tapping her toes against the floorboards. "Everyone knows my father rejected you when you were younger. If this is some cruel way of getting back at him, you should be ashamed, because this has gone too far. This is just being mean."

Ella smiled thinly. "Goldilocks, what about Hillary's shoes? What do the soles reveal?"

Hillary suddenly jumped around, as if her feet were being nipped, as if movement alone could camouflage her deeds.

"Ohh, yes, they're glowing! Do stop skipping. You look like an imbecile!" Goldilocks tilted back a little to peer at other people's feet. "And no one else's... Wait, and Axel's boots too! Look, look!" Goldilocks passed the lens to Dirk.

Hillary suddenly swung around and pointed to Axel. "He did it! He made Ace drink the unicorn blood at the cluckoo shop—I tried to stop him!"

Ella arched an eyebrow at Axel. "Perhaps you would care to explain what happened last night after you intercepted Ace's message via young Olly?"

Axel folded his arms and leaned up against the table, his back to the glasses now all filled with bright green ink. "I went to the cluckoo shop, where I saw Hillary force Ace to drink something, I don't know what, while he was held by Rooster. Neither of them saw me."

"Lies! That's not what happened!" Hillary shouted, seeking shelter at her father's side. "You know I wouldn't do that, Dad?"

"Quiet!" Goldi said, stamping a tiny foot. "You will be given a turn to talk. And I want to hear Axel's side!"

"As do I!" said Dirk, turning his tricorn around in his hands.

Axel continued, "Rooster took fright and ran off when Ace started choking and foaming at the mouth." The sheriff paused and touched his chin, as if recalling black bubbles streaming down the little craftsman's face. "I chased after Rooster for some time, but I lost him. I was a bit drunk, I confess." He sighed. "Anyway, on returning, I stumbled around in the now dark alley and bumped into Hillary just as the haberdashery twin hailed me out the window." He gestured to Millie, who nodded. Axel ran a hand through his dark hair, and a moment of regret crossed his features. "I figured instead of confronting Hillary, I'd play along and keep what I'd seen to myself until I could figure out what she was up to."

"He's clearly lying," Hillary protested. "Everyone knows he hates Cassidy because she wants his job—what possible reason would I have for hurting *anyone*?"

"Sadly, hundreds of reasons, I should think," Ella sighed, regarding the blotched banknote. "They say money, after all, is the root of all evil." She nodded to Axel. "Go on, then what happened? Why didn't you fetch help for Ace?"

Axel sighed. "After walking Hillary home, I did go back to the cluckoo shop, but it was empty. Thinking that Cassidy must have already found Ace and taken him to the doctor if that was necessary, I returned to my party, only to discover Rooster there, at the back door. He begged me to lock him up for his own safety. Said if I provided him with an alibi, he'd be my informant. Seemed like a fair deal."

"See! He admits working with criminals!" Hillary shouted.

"Speaking of admissions," Ella interjected. "You admitted you were at the cluckoo shop. Just happened to be there in the dead of night? Whatever for?"

The haberdashery twins exchanged knowing glances, and Hillary tuned into their implication. "He *lured* me—tried to take advantage of me!"

Harold's stout little chest puffed with outrage. "You dog!" the postmaster uttered, his vest buttons straining. "How dare you!"

Axel shrugged. Barely stepped back from the little man, like he might dismiss an angry squirrel. "If anyone is being taken advantage of, it's me!"

"Well, your murky reputation does rather precede you," Ella muttered wryly. "And Ace isn't the only craftsman to have met an untimely demise this year."

"That's very true," Goldi uttered aside to Dirk. "Everyone has heard the rumours that Axel killed Rum a few months ago."

Axel folded his arms across his broad chest and kicked at the floorboards. "For the record, I didn't kill Rum. He fell. I just took credit for his death to make myself look, you know, tougher."

There was a beat of awkward silence as everyone contemplated this revelation when suddenly Hillary shouted, "Lies! You can't believe a word he says! He deals with criminals every day! He's horrible—I'm nice! I work at the post office, for goodness' sake!"

"Ah, yes, the post office," Ella said. "Thank you so much for bringing that up. You see, the final thing I couldn't figure out was the source of the banknotes. Yes, the ink comes in whisky bottles via a shipment that Hillary, as a post office worker, as she so helpfully emphasised, can easily intercept. But what about the genuine one-dollar notes that were sent to be altered? Avalon currency isn't available here—all paper money is a complete novelty. Even low-value banknotes would attract attention. So how are they being slipped in across the border with no one the wiser?"

The Charmington citizens gathered within the attic office regarded each other with shrugs and blank stares, while overhead, the mechanics of the town hall clock whirred and crowed the hour.

When the din had receded into the eerie quiet, Ella said, "Tobias, would you be so kind as to step forward?"

CHAPTER 33

THE FINAL, FINAL PIECE

HORRIFIED GASPS ESCAPED FROM THE onlookers. "Sister, what is happening now?" Sally hissed to Millie, their own arguments forgotten in the unfolding drama.

"But I—I don't know anything!" Tobias, the schoolmaster, protested, running a hand through his thinning ginger hair and peering imploringly at the faces all staring back at him in wonder.

Outside, darkness had fallen, but inside, the tax office was filled with a bright rainbow glow from the charming fairy lights, making for a peculiarly conflicting atmosphere when the tension within the room was increasingly dark and stormy.

"No, of course, you don't. I wanted to talk about your attempts to get published," Ella said, her tone light and friendly in the stunned silence. "You see, I caught Hillary rifling through one of your manuscripts that your Avalon publisher Lovespell Press had returned. It struck me as a little odd. And just as peculiar, I learned today that the publisher shut down over a year ago."

"That's true!" Haberdashery twin Sally piped up. "We had so much trouble sourcing extra copies of *Cinderella* for *my* Book Club. First editions of *Cinderella* are quite valuable now."

Millie elbowed her. "Hush. Not now. Why do you always have to make everything about you?"

"Wait, what?" Tobias was aghast. "But Lovespell can't have gone out of business. I've sent them two manuscripts this year! They sent them back with editing notes. Next time...next time...they say. Nearly ready for publication!" He clenched a fist in the air, his face a picture of anguished genius. Or at least, an anguished schoolmaster suffering a midlife crisis.

Axel stood up straight, as if stung. "The publisher is a front! They smuggle the one-dollar banknotes between the pages of Tobias' stories! And then Hillary here overprints them with black magic ink! Low-value coming in, high-value going back out. Clever."

Ella nodded. "Indeed. It took me a while to put that final piece together..."

Hillary huffed a derisive breath of air. "A fine theory, but where is the proof? Did you see me with any of these banknotes?"

"No," Ella admitted, feeling the moment slipping.

"That's because I was just reading it!" Hillary suddenly grabbed Tobias' hands in her own. "You must believe me. Your words, such poetry—the romance—it makes me blush. It touches me *deeply!*"

Taken aback, Tobias gulped. A glimmer of hope passed across his confused and disappointed features, and he looked at her with desperate, pleading eyes. "Really? Which, ah, which character did you like best?"

Ella perked up. "Yes, tell Tobias—tell everybody—which one is your favourite, and we can clear up this misunderstanding."

Axel smirked. "I want to hear this."

Hillary looked abashed. "A favourite? How could I choose *one*?"

A groan escaped several lips, and people threw up their hands as comprehension rippled across all faces except for Tobias'. "Ha! She's lying. She hasn't read any of his stories," Robinne said to Willow, who nodded in agreement.

Goldilocks pointed up at Hillary. "You liar! Murderer!"

Hillary burst into tears. "But—but it's not my fault!" Now raising an accusing finger of her own, she pointed at her father and sobbed, "I only did what Dad made me do! And he's got a fake set of accounting books. He's been stealing from the post office for years!"

"Hillary..." Harold uttered. His tone of betrayal punctuated like she had stabbed him with a knife. Releasing his daughter's hand, he pulled out a desk chair and slumped down, visibly shaken.

Ella rolled her eyes. "Magic preserve me, child! Can you not maintain a shred of dignity and concede defeat?" Ella shook her head. "Your father may be fiddling the books, but you and you alone put the poison down Ace's throat. You moved Ace's body, then unfortunately for you, Cassidy shows up, so you lure her into the post office basement—she never would have been off her guard if she had followed Axel. The blueprint room is *your* little hidey-hole, not Harold's. I thought it was his drinking room, but he *doesn't* drink. Not to mention the bottles were filled with ink, not whiskey! You thought you'd have plenty of time to dispose of the bodies. If I hadn't needed to go into that room, no one would have found them. You *locked*

Cassidy in to die there!" She waved Axel forward. "Sheriff, do your duty and take her away."

Dirk echoed the sentiment. "Take her away! She poisoned Ace."

Goldilocks nodded, and her feud dissolved. "Hillary framed Cassidy! She tried to murder Cassidy too!"

The haberdashery twins joined in, waving lace hankies. "For shame!"

"Arrest her! Arrest her!" the Baker Street orphans chanted until Axel grabbed Hillary and forced her arms behind her back.

"Hillary Harper, by the power vested in me by Her Majesty, Queen Sibylla, yadda yadda, I arrest you on the suspicion of murder and grievous bodily harm with intent to cause death. You will be incarcerated in Nottingham Prison until such time as you can stand trial..."

"Don't put her in the police holding cells while awaiting transportation to Nottingham," Ella cautioned as Axel marched Hillary to the door. "You should keep her separated from Rooster."

The sheriff rolled his eyes. "How about *you* don't tell me how to do my job? Keep them separated, I ask you? It's not my first day on the job..."

Ella didn't hear what else the newly appointed sheriff said as he dragged Hillary from the room, accompanied by Robinne as a witness, because Harold suddenly leapt to his feet and shouted in her face, "How dare you! This is all your fault, you obnoxious, stupid old woman!"

Ella stepped back as Dirk and the doctor came to her aid and grabbed Harold roughly by the elbows.

"Dirk, would you mind taking Harold somewhere secure? At least until we can properly investigate his accounts ledgers," Ella added brightly. "Perhaps the castle dungeon might be a suitable location?"

"My pleasure," Dirk responded, touching his hairline in salute, the tricorn discarded upon the table.

"Unhand me!" shouted Harold, and surprising everyone with his speed, the postmaster ducked in an attempt to flee. The manoeuvre, however, only served to dislodge Harold's wig.

For a moment, there was shocked silence as everyone remaining in the room stared at the brown clump of hair on the carpet.

And then Olly swept it up and tried it on.

Dirk dragged the postmaster after his daughter, and the room suddenly felt a lot lighter, and there was a general turning away, and Ella was no longer the centre of attention. Willow offered Tobias a brownie to lift his spirits, while Doctor Hyde gave him a consoling pat, one writer to another, and small talk resumed.

"Told you it was a wig," Sally said knowingly. "That's a silver coin you owe me."

"It was I who made that bet," Millie countered, hands on hips as the article in question was passed back and forth between the giggling children. "Who did he think he was fooling with such an obvious hairpiece?"

Goldilocks pushed her way through the dissipating crowd up to Ella and said, "Take me to Cassidy. I will do my best to heal her."

CHAPTER 34

ROOSTER WRAP–UP

POLICE STATION CELLS, NORTHGATE SQUARE, CHARMINGTON.

A short time later, having directed Goldi and her magical healing abilities to the Hot Cockle Lane Hospital, accompanied by Doctor Hyde, Ella snuck back into the new police station. She paused outside the old wine cellar door. Would Axel have done as advised and kept Hillary and Rooster apart so they couldn't corroborate another story?

A crash came from somewhere upstairs, in the rooms that once used to accommodate guests of the inn, followed by Hillary cursing and swearing. Ella shrugged. She had her answer. Opening the door, she made her way down into the former wine cellars, now the police station lock-up.

"You followed the money?" Rooster voiced from the shadows in the back of the cellar as Ella approached the bars of his cell with her walking-stick light held aloft.

"Yes, I did, thank you. It was a good tip."

Rooster touched his hand to his forehead, as if tipping a hat, but otherwise seemed unmoved. He slunk down, his back pressed to the stone walls. "Then she must have got what she wanted…"

"There was one tiny detail that has eluded me…" Ella clasped her hands about the bars of the locked cell door. "Why did Hillary move Ace to the post office?"

"She what?" Rooster turned. "She did what? That wasn't our plan!"

"My thoughts exactly. Why draw attention to somewhere that *indicated* her?" Ella hummed while thinking. "Hillary thought Cassidy was dead. She wasn't to know that Cassidy would survive. It's almost as if she was setting up *another* person with keys to the post office. At first, I thought it must be her father alone—clearly, she wanted him out of the way."

"Aye," Rooster nodded. "Follow the money, like I told you! You ain't find the ledgers?" But then he clamped his mouth shut, as if remembering whose side he was meant to be on. Then he sighed, resigned. "Plan went out the window anyways. When the little guy showed up unexpectedly last night. No one shoulda got hurt—but she panicked. Or so I thought... Stay in the shadows, don't draw attention..." he mumbled to himself, as if repeating instructions.

"Ah! Of course, with her father out of the way, Hillary could step up this counterfeiting scheme you are embroiled in..." One theory confirmed, Ella continued. "But then there was the question of the lost keys. Hillary claimed to have lost not one, but *two* keys. Therefore, could there be a person who she had inexplicably given a *spare* post office key? A person no one trusted? An ideal scapegoat *if* her plan to oust her father went astray?"

Rooster slapped his hand to his shirt front, hooked a finger to the chain at his neck and drew out a key, then he laughed. "She set me up. The vixen!" He sighed again. "I didn't want nothing to do with this. I just wanted a fresh start." He clenched his fist around the brass key. "But there ain't no out once you're in. No one escapes the missus."

"I take it you're referring to Mrs. Haversham. She is the true mastermind behind this scheme. I assume the counterfeit one-hundreds end up in Nottingham to aid her there. Does she think she can buy her way out of prison?"

Startled, Rooster got to his feet. "You work for her, too? Then I'm done for..."

Ella thinned her lips. "Quite the opposite. Mrs. Haversham is in Nottingham Prison, thanks to me."

"You! So, you're the one. The missus got a terrible hatred for you!" Rooster threw himself at the bars at Ella's feet. "That makes us allies. Please, I'll do anyfing."

Ella tutted. "I wish I could believe you, Mr. Rooster, but in my experience, people soon fall back into old ways without proper motivation to stay on the straight and narrow."

"I can't go back to the prison. She'll kill me soon as spit! You know she will. I just need a fresh start, need to break my bad luck."

Ella held up a finger to hush him as light footsteps tapped down the wooden ramp, and a pair of yellow duckie boots appeared, accompanied by Gretel, who was grumbling about the unprofess-ionalism of leaving someone still alive while on their deathbed.

Rooster's eyes bulged wide. "That—that's the vam—the vamp—! No, no, no..." He whimpered, then stuffed his knuckles to his mouth and bit down. Pleading eyes looked up at Ella, tears rolling down his cheeks.

Ella nodded grimly at the whimpering criminal and flourished a hand at the little blonde girl. "Rooster, may I introduce Gretel—or as I like to think, the proper motivation..."

Gretel's eyes likewise widened on spying the terrified criminal, now curled in a ball at the farthest corner of the cell. She gripped the bars and shook the door. "Hey! You! You set my business on fire! Come closer so I can kill you!" She gave the bars another shake, and then snapped at Ella, "Open zis door! Right now!"

Ella folded her arms. "How about a game of hide and go seek?"

Gretel narrowed her eyes and twirled a small finger around one of her pigtails. "Ja, okay, I'm listening. I vin, I get to eat big chicken, *ja*?"

"No, no, no!" wailed Rooster. "Please, I swear I'll be no more trouble, I swear. Don't let her get me!"

"Rooster," said Ella, "I'm going to grant your wish and give you a fresh start. I'm going to let you go—"

"No, no, no! I changed my mind. I like it in here! I want to stay!"

"Let you go," Ella repeated, "on the condition that you *never* set foot in Wyld Kingdom again. You will no longer blame luck on poor decisions. Instead, you will *make better* decisions." Ella turned to Gretel. "My dear, would you please stand back from the door? That's lovely. Close your eyes and count down from fifty."

"Fifty. Forty-nine—"

"Help!" shouted Rooster. "Somebody save me!"

Ella clasped her hands about the iron bars and pulled. The lock clicked open, and the door swung wide. "Lawks, how did that happen?" She held out her palm. "Key, please."

"Forty-two, forty-von, forty—"

Rooster cast one horrified glance at Gretel with her hands over her eyes and then yanked off the keychain from around his neck. He bolted past Ella, shunting her out of the way, running so fast the key had only just hit the floor, his scream still echoing about the chamber when he reached the top of the stairs.

"How rude," Ella muttered. "He nearly knocked me over. That was uncalled for."

Gretel stopped counting and bobbed a curtsey. "Highness." She ran after him, calling out in a sing-song voice, "Here I come! Ready or not!"

Ella dusted her hands. "Right, then, that's sorted. One more thing to take care of..."

CHAPTER 35

ELLA'S SHOCKING DECISION

CHARITY HOSPITAL, HOT COCKLE LANE, CHARMINGTON.

A few hours later, Ella found herself tip-toeing through the rows of hospital beds for the third time that day. Despite her concerns earlier, the old warehouse space at night time was less gloomy than anticipated. The large space was warm. Ella could feel heat radiating up from the stone floor. Someone had strung up a few strands of fairy lights, and their soft golden hue added to the air of serenity. Most of the patients appeared to be sleeping peacefully, despite Marge the midwife's extremely loud snoring, and Ella wondered if Goldilocks had spread more of her magical healing abilities across the other patients. Then again, it was clear that Doctor Hyde was a competent man, so their well-being was just as likely due to his care.

Nigella Pickford was awake and sitting up, taking advantage of a curl of fairy lights strung across her bedframe, and appeared entranced deep within the pages of the decades-old copy of the *Charmington Chatter*.

Ella offered the actress the day's copy of the *Nottingham Times* that she had taken from the castle library after visiting her old bed chambers located high up in the East Tower. "My apologies for the late delivery."

"Thank you, Your Ladyship," Nigella said in a low voice, and then glanced at the newspaper headline. *Merlin's World Book Tour!* "Oh, fabulous! I'm such a fan. Do you think he'll visit Charmington, too?"

"Unfortunately," Ella conceded with a whisper. It seemed unavoidable that she must encounter her brother sometime next month. Still, perhaps she would be so busy with tax matters that she could make excuses not to attend whatever events were undoubtedly planned to be held in his honour. Bidding the actress good night, Ella crept across the distance to Cassidy's bedside.

The young guardswoman and Tomcat appeared to be having a pleasant conversation. They were laughing and smiling, and Ella swallowed down her impulse to tell Tom off for risking exposing his magical secret. After all, it was refreshing to see them both in good spirits after the terrible day.

They stopped talking as Ella approached. "Don't mind me," she said, perching on an empty cot beside Cassidy. She placed several letters for Tom from Master Spicer that had been in the P.O. box among the bundle she had collected on the end of Cassidy's bed and then ripped open the golden invitation from Prince John. "Thank goodness the coronation isn't for months!" She set the invite aside. It was a problem for much later.

"We thought you must have gone home," Tomcat said, sitting up straight, his little pink ears twitching.

Ella shrugged. "Not yet. I thought I should take advantage of my fully-functioning knees, and I went to my castle chambers at the top of East Tower to collect a few items and store them in the tax office…"

"Like your crown collection?" Cassidy joked. "Bags of jewels?"

Ella arched an eyebrow. "Something like that. I own a rather fancy square of carpet." She glanced around the darkened space and up at the snow melt from the roof tiles that dripped constantly *blip blip* into nearby buckets. "It might be sold to improve conditions here or to pay for more staffing. I will let the doctor decide." She smiled at the young woman. The colour had returned to Cassidy's cheeks, and her eyes were bright and focused. "I take it Goldilocks has worked her magic on you? All better?"

Cassidy nodded and idly tickled Tomcat under his chin. "All better…" she said, but her words were edged with regret. No doubt she was reflecting that her trusted friend and colleague, Ace, had not been so lucky.

"That reminds me," Ella said, setting the invitation aside and standing up so she could better reach into her skirt pocket. "I have Ace's rose spectacles. You will want to return them to his family…" Ella's fingers quested around the pocket. Empty? What was this? Had she mistakenly put them in the other pocket, along with the vial? No… Ella patted her cloak pockets, and then realisation dawned.

"Ugh! He picked my pocket! That wretch!" Ella stamped her foot. "I showed him mercy and he darn well picked my pocket!" She sat back down on the thin mattress with a thump and folded her arms, wondering what the chances were that Gretel had caught up with Rooster. The fellow had a fair turn of speed when he had the mind, and knowing Gretel was on his tail would no doubt lend him wings.

"So, what were you two discussing? Did Tom explain how he figured out Hillary's scheming?"

Tomcat ducked his head, green cat eyes lowered. "I told Cassidy how *you* figured out Hillary was planning on eventually dobbing in her dad for keeping two sets of accounts book, and that her plans to test out the printing press were interrupted when Ace's spectacles alerted him to the glow of black magic."

"Nonsense," Ella huffed, still ruminating on the sting of Rooster having stolen the precious spectacles, "it was a team effort. Tom figured out as much as I."

Cassidy tousled his furry head and said, "Well, Rookie, we might make a proper guardsman out of you yet." Tomcat's whiskers fanned in a halo of pride, and he puffed out his chest.

"Right, I'll be off. Now I know you are feeling better, I'll leave the two of you alone. I'm sure you have lots of things to discuss."

"I'll walk you home," Tomcat said. He pointed to a few beds over, where Ella realised Dirk Turpin was tucked up under blankets. "Goldi put Dirk to sleep. She said it's the best way to counter the ill effects of the exposure to the black magic tainted notes. So he can't drive you home in the carriage."

Ella chuckled. "That is very kind, but I collected some transport when I went back to my rooms. Robinne is practising with it outside now. Learning to take the corners is tricky."

"I'll walk you to the door, then," Tomcat said, leaping off the bed. As they walked across the large, cavernous space, he added, "Do you really think Mrs. Haversham orchestrated the whole counterfeiting operation from prison?"

Ella shrugged. "I do. She is a smart and devious woman. And unicorn blood was her signature ingredient whenever she delved into black magic."

"But what would she do with money when she's stuck in prison?"

"Bribes." Ella shrugged. "Her post box was filled with competition entries. Perhaps Hillary is told who to send the fake money to as prizes. To people Haversham wants to curry favour." Ella shuddered. One day, Mrs. Haversham would have served her time, and she would be released. That was a day Ella dreaded. She gave herself a mental shake. That day was not today, nor was it tomorrow. But one day, one day, Ella would have to face that hateful old witch again.

"Good night, Ella," Tomcat said, pausing at the threshold of the hospital. "Thank you for saving Cass. You really came through for me."

Ella felt a sting of emotion well up in her eyes. "That's what friends do." Really, she wasn't normally so emotional! It must be due to the late hour. It had been a very long day.

"I can't see Robinne?" Tomcat uttered, peering from the steps of the hospital into the dim gas lamp-lit street of Hot Cockle Lane. His breath fanned in the frosty night air.

"Look up. I told her to practise flying around a bit. The speed takes some getting used to."

"Flying?" Tomcat darted out on the street as something rectangular swooshed out of the darkness and swooped past in a gust of sandalwood-scented air. "What was that?" Tomcat's hackles rose.

"That is a rather ostentatious gift given to me many years ago from my sister Arabella and the sultan of Constantinople," Ella said, squinting up into the inky sky peppered with stars. "I'm not fond of heights, so I left it at the castle when I moved to the cottage. It's called a flying carpet."

Tomcat's mouth fell open and sharp little canines gaped up at her. "But that's magic! Ella, magic is banned on pain of death!"

Ella shrugged. "Not next month, according to the queen's decree. And after that, I rather think they'll have to catch me!" She winked down at Tom, who ducked as Robinne on the rectangle of red and gold carpet swooshed past again, squealing with a mix of terror and delight. "Then again, I will probably sell it. It's worth quite a lot, and Doctor Hyde will put the funds to better use."

Ella stood, hands on hips, and looked back into the glow of the Charity Hospital. "Today really reminded me of what Charmington has lost. Doctor Hyde is a capable chap, but without magic, our people suffer needless pain, and I for one am not going to sit idly by any longer. Magic has always done more good than harm. If I hadn't lost my powers, I would have been able to heal Cassidy today! But I couldn't, and I felt useless and helpless. So magic help me, I am jolly well going to earn my wand back because the world needs magic!"

Tomcat blinked up at Ella. "Wow! How are you going to do that?"

Ella's mind drifted back to the children she had spoken to today, and to the beginner magical textbooks that Merlin had sent, and she smiled. "I am going to teach."

~ The End ~

NEXT IN SERIES

MERLIN AND THE KILLER CRUSH

What is the dark secret behind the haberdashery sister's feud?

Coincidence or curse? The month Queen Sibylla lifts the ban on magic, Merlin loses his powers and one of the haberdashery sisters loses her life!

Ella and Tomcat are soon on the case and must uncover what a spate of typewriter thefts and the true identity of an infamous romance author have in common.

Blackmail, **poisoned pens** and **secrets** cause chaos in *'Merlin and the Killer Crush'* book 4 in the Wyld Enchantment Woods Paranormal Cozy mystery series.

Out Soon!

Follow Kura Jane Carpenter Amazon author page to stay up to date with all titles in the series.
https://www.amazon.com/stores/Kura-Jane-Carpenter/author/B0BGT43WSR

Acknowledgements

Special Thanks to All Readers who take the time to Post a Review – I simply cannot continue without your support in sharing the word.

Another great debt of Appreciation is owed to **Kevin Berry** for **proofreading**, and **Charlotte Kieft** for **copyediting**.

A very big Thank You to my lovely beta readers, in particular **Kay Mercer, Angela Oliver** and **Alice Carpenter** your feedback as always was invaluable.

In addition, I would like to offer my heartfelt thanks to the kind *ARC Readers* of Book 1 & 2. Your reviews are truly appreciated!

About the Author

Kura Jane Carpenter is a New Zealand author and was the 2019 recipient of the Sir Julius Vogel award for Best New Talent. When not writing, Kura enjoys convincing strangers that greyhounds make the best pets.

Web: **www.kuracarpenter.com**

Instagram: @kura.carpenter

BookBub: https://www.bookbub.com/authors/kura-jane-carpenter

Amazon Author Profile: https://www.amazon.com/stores/Kura-Jane-Carpenter/author/B0BGT43WSR

Link Tree: https://linktr.ee/kurajane